A brittle tension gripped the room as Paige sat up and flexed her fingers. She hesitated, and then boldly thrust out her hand. "Remote!"

Leo frowned when nothing happened. A moment later the remote control slowly dissolved into orb particles, which drifted into Paige's hand and slowly re-formed. At first glance the device seemed fine. On closer inspection, she noticed that the lettering formed nonsense words and the buttons were out of line. "Oh, boy," she winced. "That's definitely worse than yesterday."

"Which is what I wanted to find out." Leo kept his tone matter-of-fact when the three sisters looked to him for clarification. "Something happened to start the power drain in the first place, and whatever it was, it happened to each of you again since yesterday."

The girls looked baffled. "Nothing happened," Paige insisted.

"Yes, it did," Leo said firmly. "Nothing else can account for the diminished powers and the excessive physical and emotional side effects you're all experiencing. You've all encountered something in the past few days that you've never run into before.

"And whatever [   ]ct with it twice."

Charmed™

Published by Simon & Schuster

DARK VENGEANCE

A novelization by Diana G. Gallagher

Based on the hit TV Series created by

Constance M. Burge

SIMON PULSE
New York London Toronto Sydney Singapore

With love for John Alan Streb:
friend, son-in-law,
and all round great guy

First Simon Pulse edition November 2002
™ & © 2002 Spelling Television Inc. All Rights Reserved.

SIMON PULSE
An imprint of Simon & Schuster
Children's Publishing Division
1230 Avenue of the Americas
New York, NY 10020

The text of this book was set in Palatino.

Printed in the United States of America

10 9 8 7 6 5 4 3 2 1

Library of Congress Control Number 2002111612

ISBN 0-689-85079-4

DARK VENGEANCE

Chapter

1

"Those socks don't match." Phoebe Halliwell sat on the bed, watching her fiancé, Cole Turner, pack. As usual, she had no idea where he was going or how long he'd be gone. However, she didn't give him a hard time about taking off for parts unknown, frequently and without notice. Surviving the death of his demon half required more than a casual adjustment.

"They don't?" Cole stared at the socks in his hand—one blue and one tan—as though pairing socks of identical color did not matter.

Which it doesn't, Phoebe thought. Compared to the trauma of becoming suddenly human, matching socks rated way below trivial on the what-matters scale.

Flopping onto her side, Phoebe braced her chin in her hand. She knew that if she lost her powers with no hope of getting them back, she

1

wouldn't be able to just accept it either. She'd feel ineffectual and incomplete—and cheated out of something precious and irreplaceable.

She had no right to complain because he needed time alone, Phoebe reminded herself. She had mixed the power-stripping potion that Emma, a young woman who wanted revenge for her dead husband, had used to kill Belthazor. Cole insisted that he didn't blame her, but she felt responsible anyway.

Cole shrugged and dropped the balled pair of mismatched socks into his canvas duffel. "Won't matter where I'm going."

"It won't?" Phoebe asked, startled by the unexpected opening into taboo territory. Since Cole was struggling with an identity crisis, she usually respected his right to privacy. This time she decided to press. "Why not?"

Cole hesitated, then glanced back with a mischievous grin. "I think trout are color-blind."

"You're going fishing?" Phoebe sat up.

She had envisioned Cole holed up in some cheap, seedy motel on his recent excursions to "find himself." She had assumed these periods of isolated reflection included self-indulgent sulking over lost magic balanced by profound remorse for Belthazor's evil deeds. It had never occurred to her that he might be having *fun* while he was coming to terms with being a powerless human.

"I might." Cole tossed his other pair of blue and tan socks into the bag and zipped it closed.

"I've heard that sitting in a boat drowning a skewered worm for the perverse pleasure of luring a hungry fish to death by suffocation helps people think."

"That's a warped but apt description of a popular pastime." Phoebe grimaced.

"Sorry. Must be residual demon effects that haven't worn off yet." Cole kissed her on the forehead and smiled.

Phoebe cuffed his arm and cocked a playful eyebrow. "You really miss being dangerous, don't you?"

"Maybe," Cole conceded, "but I'm working on it."

"I'm not worried," Phoebe said. "No evil guy would *ever* wear blue and tan socks."

"How long before I'm off the hook for this fashion faux pas?" Cole frowned. "No pun intended."

"It's already forgotten." Phoebe held up her hand as though swearing an oath. "Not another word. Just come back safe and soon."

"You can count on it." Cole touched her face, his smile tight. "I have to go."

Phoebe nodded and followed him down the stairs. Despite Cole's assurances, she couldn't shake the feeling that he was holding something back. However, she was determined not to let her imagination run wild. His secret might be something as simple and harmless as hating the scent of her shampoo—or not.

"When does your computer class at the community college start?" Cole paused in the doorway to pull his car keys from his pocket.

"Tonight." Phoebe smiled, pleased that he remembered she had signed up to take a course in Web site design.

"I'm a little nervous, though," Phoebe admitted. "My computer skills are pretty basic."

"Isn't that why you're taking this course?" Cole asked. "To improve?"

"And to make a few bucks," Phoebe replied. "With luck."

An amused sparkle played in Cole's brown eyes. "I bet you'll be a dot-com zillionaire in no time."

"Don't think so!" Phoebe exclaimed with mock horror. "Dot-com zillionaires have become so rare, they're almost extinct."

"Extinction is not an option." Cole bent his head, drawing Phoebe into a long, lingering kiss. "I'll be back in a few days."

"I'll be waiting." Smiling, Phoebe watched until Cole pulled his car away from the curb. The instant she closed the door, the house felt empty.

"Is Cole coming down for breakfast?" Piper asked her sister as Phoebe came into the kitchen.

"No, he just left." Phoebe grabbed a glass and opened the refrigerator.

"Again?" Paige Matthews looked up from the morning paper.

"Are you done with the sports section?" Leo asked over the rim of his coffee cup.

Piper flashed her youngest sibling a warning glance. Focused on Phoebe, Paige handed Leo the sports pages and totally missed Piper's unspoken message.

"Where did he go this time?" Paige asked with clueless curiosity.

Piper sighed as she folded Leo's omelette. Paige wasn't heartless or mean. She was just as new to being a sister as she was to being a witch. Raised as an only child, Paige couldn't always tell when uncomfortable family topics should be avoided.

Like now, Piper thought as she lifted the frying pan and picked up a plate. Five minutes after Cole departed for who-knew-where for who-knew-what purpose was not a good time to discuss his absences, even though Phoebe didn't seem to mind.

Distracted, Piper slid the hot omelette out of the pan onto her thumb. "Ouch!"

Leo's attention instantly shifted from yesterday's scores to his injured wife. "Are you okay?"

Nodding, Piper dropped the pan back on the burner, the plate on the counter, and stuck her thumb in her mouth. She gingerly retrieved the toast that had just popped up and dropped the pieces on the plate.

"Cole went fishing." Phoebe answered Paige as she poured OJ into her glass.

"Really?" Paige's eyes widened with surprise. "Cole never struck me as the fishing type. It's so . . . stationary."

Piper noted the younger woman's pointed sarcasm. Paige hadn't trusted Cole since she'd found out he had spent the last century leading a double life as a demon. She apparently didn't realize that her lack of faith in his redemption hurt Phoebe. However, for the sake of domestic tranquillity, Phoebe usually let the verbal barbs pass.

"Is that omelette almost done, Piper?" Leo asked suddenly. "I'm starved."

"Not a good idea to rush the cook, Leo." Annoyed, Piper buttered his toast. Then she realized that her Whitelighter husband had been trying to change the subject away from Cole's uncharacteristic fishing trip.

Unfortunately, Paige wasn't picking up on the cues. Like a political pundit on prime-time TV, she kept talking undeterred, locked into her own agenda.

"I mean, how dull compared with skiing or rock climbing or white-water rafting," Paige said.

Piper set Leo's breakfast on the table. "Don't get too used to this, Mr. Wyatt. My gourmet omelettes are an occasional wifely indulgence, not a required domestic duty."

"Uh-huh." Leo frowned, not sure if Piper's remark was in jest. "Are you serious?"

"Completely." Grabbing her coffee mug off the counter, Piper sank into a chair and fixed Paige with a hard stare.

Paige scowled under the scrutiny. "What's wrong with you this morning, Piper?"

"Monday morning blahs? Everyone seems to be a little tense," Leo observed.

"There's nothing wrong with me that a two-week Caribbean cruise wouldn't cure," Piper quipped. She turned to Phoebe. "Is Cole fishing for anything in particular?"

Piper hoped she sounded casually interested and not suspicious. Phoebe had learned a valuable lesson when she had lied about killing Cole—a.k.a. Belthazor—after they first discovered his true identity: She would not betray her sisters to protect him again. If something about him threatened their safety or their mission as the Charmed Ones, Phoebe wouldn't hesitate to tell.

"You might want to dig out your recipes for trout." Phoebe put the juice carton back on the shelf and closed the refrigerator door. "In case he actually catches something."

"I'll do that." Piper raised her cup and paused. "When is he coming back?"

"I'm not sure." Phoebe sat down. "A few days."

Piper exhaled with relief. "Good, because I'm way too busy to mess with fresh fish for dinner tonight."

"Better for me, too," Phoebe said. When everyone turned to stare, she added, "that Cole won't be here tonight."

"What could possibly be more important than being with the tall, dark, and dastardly love of your life?" Paige asked.

"Nothing," Phoebe said. "It's just that my Web site class starts at seven."

"Oh, right. I forgot." Piper held up crossed fingers. "Let's hope you have a knack."

Piper and her sisters never knew when the Power of Three might be needed to save an innocent from some horrendous supernatural evil. Consequently, Piper didn't want Phoebe tied down to a nine-to-five job.

Being confined by employment wasn't a problem for Piper, because she owned P3. Running the popular local nightclub was demanding, but she had complete freedom of movement.

Bob Cowan, Paige's boss at South Bay Social Services, grumbled occasionally, but Paige could usually come and go as her Charmed duties required. The chances that Phoebe would find a job with the necessary flexibility and an understanding boss were remote to nonexistent.

"A freelance business in Web site design sounds like the perfect career for a witch on twenty-four/seven demon call," Paige said.

"Since I'm obviously not going anywhere with my psychology degree." Phoebe sighed.

"Some extra cash coming in would be nice." Piper glanced at the pile of bills collecting on the hutch. No matter what else happened today— invasion of fever fiends, ambush by spit sprites, or an insidious plague of skin mold—she had to deal with the household finances. The money available for Halliwell Manor's operating expenses was always stretched thin, and she didn't want to incur any budget-busting late charges.

"Ditto that." Paige lifted her handbag off the floor. The leather around the metal clasp was scorched. "My meager wardrobe funds can't keep up with the demon damage."

"Let's see if I can get through the course first, okay?" Phoebe exhaled long and loud. "I don't take to technology as naturally as I do magic."

"You're going to ace the course," Paige said. "And who knows? Phoebe's Web Enterprises might be the beginning of a new dot-com boom."

"Not likely, but thanks for the vote of confidence." Phoebe sighed. "Anyway, it'll be easier to concentrate the first few days without Cole around to distract me."

"Speaking of distractions"—Leo pushed his empty plate aside and leaned toward Piper—"I thought you might want to—"

"Not!" Piper's tone was sharper than she had intended. She *did* feel a little guilty about having neglected Leo lately, but she didn't want to discuss it in front of her sisters. "No time for fun and games today, Leo."

"You can't be *that* busy," Phoebe teased.

"No?" Piper counted on her fingers as she rattled off the items on her schedule. "I've got to catch up the bills, iron Leo's shirts, grocery shop, and audition a new band for next weekend because Rock Bottom cancelled. Plus, there's a huge delivery arriving at P3 this afternoon that has to be stocked before we open."

"That's why I thought you might want some help," Leo said. "I can do the grocery shopping and—"

Piper cut him off with a you've-got-to-be-kidding look. "The last time you went to the grocery store you came back with cabbage instead of iceberg lettuce."

Leo threw up his arms in frustration. "I was in a hurry."

"And considering that we're still talking about it six months later," Phoebe said, "that's a mistake he's not likely to repeat."

"Maybe not, but I'm a chef, and chefs are very particular about the quality of their groceries." Piper wasn't in the mood to be gracious. Eating shrimp cocktail served on a bed of fresh cabbage hadn't bothered anyone else, but they didn't share her professional culinary sensibilities. "Especially produce."

"Sounds to me like you could use some fun

and games, Piper." Paige drained her coffee cup and rose to refill it. "If you don't lighten up, you're going to worry yourself sick and drive the rest of us nuts."

"This stuff won't get done by itself," Piper snapped. Since she had just rejected Leo's offer to help out, she instantly regretted the remark. When had she gotten so cranky? Maybe she *was* pushing herself too hard.

"But where is it written that you have to do everything, Piper?" Phoebe's brown eyes darkened with concern. "We should all pitch in. We've got time, and we're not incompetent."

"Just leafy vegetable challenged," Paige added. She ducked when Leo wadded his paper napkin and tossed it at her. "Sorry. Couldn't resist."

"Not funny." Piper took a large swallow of coffee expecting it to be warm and gagged on the cold, bitter brew. Sputtering with disgust, she set the mug down too hard. Coffee splashed onto the clean tablecloth. "Now look what I did!"

"It's just a tablecloth." Paige handed Piper a fistful of napkins. "Take it easy, okay?"

"Really, Piper." Phoebe leaned forward, drawing her flustered sister's gaze. "You're so stressed out about the small stuff, you might not be able to cope when the pressure is really on."

Piper started to protest, then nodded. Phoebe was right. Vanquishing evil was difficult and dangerous when they were all on top of their game. If one of them cracked, things could get fatal fast.

"So here's what we're going to do," Phoebe continued. "I'll iron Leo's shirts while you do the bills."

"And I'll help you stock the P3 delivery," Leo said.

"Okay." Piper nodded, her smile sincere. She wished she had words to express her gratitude, but she had never been much for verbal gushing. Some homemade chocolate-chip cookies would get the message across.

"You'll have to handle the audition yourself, but maybe Paige can stop by the store on her way home from work." Phoebe glanced over her shoulder.

Paige just stared back, speechless as she held Phoebe's questioning gaze. She couldn't believe Piper needed a favor on a day when she had to refuse.

"Is that a problem?" Phoebe pressed.

Piper held up her right hand. "I promise not to banish you to the basement if the tomatoes are bruised."

"No, that's not—I mean, I would if I could"— Paige stammered and cleared her throat—"but I can't."

"Big date?" Piper asked.

"I wish, but no such luck." Paige sighed. "My social calendar is depressingly uncluttered."

"Something evil we should know about?" Phoebe frowned.

"Only if poverty counts." Paige set the coffeepot

back on the warmer. The timing of the household crisis couldn't have been worse. Considering the less than cordial beginnings of their relationship, she and her older sister had grown very close. She hated having to beg off when Piper needed her. "I'm working the dinner shift at the Fifth Street Shelter."

"Didn't you work there last week?" Leo asked.

Paige nodded. "Yeah, but Doug was short-handed this week, too."

"So you volunteered again." Piper stuffed the coffee-soaked napkins into her mug. "Sounds like I'm not the only one who's working too hard."

"Maybe you should take your own advice, Paige," Phoebe said. "Don't you have enough to do with a full-time job and demon demolition?"

"It's only for one more week," Paige insisted. "Doug found some new people, but he needs someone with experience around to show them the ropes."

"I'm sure Doug Wilson has plenty of volunteers who know the shelter's routine, Paige," Piper said. "You're the only Fifth Street regular who has to risk life and limb to keep the world safe from evil creeps with magical powers."

"Yeah, but I can't tell Doug that," Paige countered. She had chosen a career in social work because she wanted to help others: families that had fallen on hard times, the mentally and physically disabled, and those who just couldn't seem to catch a break. Being exposed to the horrors that malevolent supernatural evil tried to inflict on the world had made her even more sensitive to ordinary human misery. She simply couldn't turn her back on the less fortunate when she could make a difference.

Phoebe fixed Paige with a no-nonsense stare. "You can't single-handedly save every unfortunate in the mortal world, either."

"Maybe not, but I can try." *Beginning with poor, old Stanley Addison*, Paige thought as she picked up her handbag and headed out the door.

Chapter

2

"Where are you, Leo?" Piper tucked the phone under her chin and glanced at the clock under the bar as she finished drying a large pitcher. "I'm expecting the delivery truck any minute."

"Sorry, but the toilet in the upstairs bathroom overflowed," Leo explained.

"How did *that* happen?" Piper asked, but she could guess. Paige used toilet paper for everything from blowing her nose to blotting her lipstick. She disposed of it in the toilet bowl and let the soggy wads collect to limit flushes and save water. The conservation effort was commendable, but the old plumbing couldn't handle it. Piper had explained the problem, but Paige hadn't broken the habit yet.

"Don't know, but it made a huge mess." Leo sounded as exasperated as Piper felt. "A few minutes ago it was high tide in the upstairs hall."

Piper groaned and turned her back to the stage, where the band was unpacking their gear. She spoke softly so her voice wouldn't carry in the empty club. "What's that going to cost?"

"Nothing," Leo assured her. "I used the plunger and got the toilet unclogged. I'll be there as soon as I finish mopping up."

"Just don't make a dramatic entrance," Piper cautioned, referring to orbing, the Whitelighter's instantaneous mode of transportation.

"With a Vengeance is setting up to audition," Piper explained. Although Leo seemed to know when the coast was clear to orb, they'd had a few close calls. Some magical events were easy to explain to mortal witnesses. People coalescing out of swirls of sparkling light wasn't one of them.

"Whatever happened to names like the Star Lighters?" Leo asked, but he didn't expect Piper to answer. "What kind of band are they?"

"According to Mason Hobbs, alternative Celtic," Piper said. "Whatever that is."

Piper dropped the damp bar rag in the sink and looked toward the stage. She had been using this booking agent since opening the club, and Mason had never let her down. She hoped this wouldn't be the first time.

With a Vengeance was new to the San Francisco area and willing to work at a reasonable rate while they established a local rep. They had also been available on short notice to replace

Rock Bottom. Composed of three handsome young men and a gorgeous young woman, the group looked hot enough to fit in with P3's clientele. If people could dance to their music, Piper wouldn't hesitate to give them the three-day gig.

Karen Ashley, a tall blonde with blue eyes and fair, flawless skin, picked up a primitive round drum. Holding an eight-inch-long stick with rounded ends, she moved her wrist in a fast up-and-down motion. Both ends of the stick alternately struck the drum, creating a rolling rhythm that conjured images of ancient warriors.

Karen adjusted the tautness of the drum's head, then set the instrument on a wooden rack. As she shoved the stick into her back pocket, she caught Piper's eye and smiled with a curt nod. "It's called a bodhran."

"Oh." Piper nodded back, her smile strained. The drum demonstration had been impressive, but somehow she couldn't picture the cool club crowd getting into a primal groove. At least not one that lasted through four sets.

"We'll be ready in a couple of minutes," Karen said.

"Whenever. Just start playing. I'll hear you." Piper's tight smile vanished as she turned her back again. "My day's not getting a whole lot better, Leo," she whispered into the phone. "Could you hurry?"

"Fifteen minutes," Leo said. "Half an hour tops. Relax, okay?"

"Don't push it, Leo." Piper hung up, closed her eyes, and took several deep breaths.

How was she supposed to relax when one thing after another had gone wrong all day? Since she had forgotten to mail the reorder form for checks, she had run out before she had paid all the bills. Going to the bank to purchase money orders had delayed her arrival at P3. Although she had gotten to the club before the band, she hadn't expected to spend time wiping down the bar. The bottles and glassware were supposed to be cleaned at closing, but last night's bartender had locked up as soon as the last customer was out the door. Dixie had left a note apologizing because her emergency baby-sitter was a high school girl with a strict curfew.

The way my luck is running, it isn't likely that Dixie's regular sitter will be back on the job tonight, Piper thought as she slid the last stemmed glass onto a suspended rack. At least Dixie had found a substitute sitter and had shown up for work. All things considered, that was a truckload of good fortune.

"Are you sure you won't have a seat, Piper?" Karen asked. Her low, sultry voice held just a hint of Irish inflection. "We're ready to have a go."

"Perfect timing." Piper wiped her hands on

her jeans. The bar chores were done, and the delivery truck was late. That's all the excuse she needed to sit down with a soda.

"You'll love us." Daniel Knowles adjusted the boom microphone over his keyboard. He was average in height and muscular with curly dark hair, and his dazzling smile and twinkling brown eyes gave him a larger-than-life aura. "Everybody does."

The ladies will definitely love Daniel, Piper thought as she filled a glass with ice and ginger ale from the bar spray gun. For some inexplicable reason, arrogance worked for good-looking musicians.

"Where did you play before San Francisco?" Piper sat down and propped her feet on a small, cylindrical table.

"In Kenny's—" The bass player, a somber brooding type called Lancer Dunne, scowled when the drummer jumped in.

"Kennebunkport." Brodie Sparks tossed his head to flip back a shock of red hair that fell over one eye. His sensuous mouth hovered on the brink of a smile that never quite happened. Tanned and freckled, his expression suggested a carefree bad boy with a mischievous sense of humor. "And other harbor towns up and down the northeastern coast."

"You're a long way from Maine," Piper said, not quite believing the shtick. She didn't know if Kenny's was a neighborhood bar or someone's garage. If the band could play, she didn't care.

"That's the truth," Lancer said. He fingered a quick riff on the heavy bass strings, then moved back as Karen stepped up to the center mike.

Daniel and Brodie gave the blond beauty their undivided attention too. Piper didn't have to guess who was in charge.

"Would you hand me my flute, Piper?" Karen pointed at a wooden case lying on the table between Piper and the stage.

"Sure." Piper got up, but she wasn't pleased. If she hired With a Vengeance, she'd have to make it clear that the job didn't come with gofer perks.

Piper lifted the wooden flute out of the velvet-lined case, noting that it looked like an antique. The delicate design carved into the burnished wood scrolled around the airholes, incorporating them into the pattern. The craftsmanship was superb.

"Thanks." Karen smiled as she stooped and wrapped her hand around the flute.

Piper suddenly felt light-headed. She let go of the instrument and gripped the edge of the stage, but the sensation passed quickly. As she walked back to her seat, she realized she hadn't eaten anything except toast for breakfast. A handful of bar peanuts would solve that problem.

After the audition, Piper thought as Karen played a long, low, sorrowful note. Food seemed unimportant as she sat back down to listen.

The melancholy sound seemed to penetrate the core of Piper's being, touching the deep sadness that lingered in the wake of Prue's death. The disturbing sense of despair that momentarily overwhelmed her retreated as the flute shifted into the frolicking strains of an Irish jig.

"Much better." Piper raised her soda glass in salute, then settled back with a contented sigh. She chuckled to herself, wondering why she let so many inconsequential things get to her. Piper, Paige, and Leo had been right to point out that her self-imposed stress was dangerous and counterproductive. Life was way too short to spend so much of it being harried and angry.

Although the folk tune was completely inappropriate for P3, the lilting melody gave Piper's spirits a much-needed lift. Smiling and tapping her foot, she decided to sit through the rest of the audition to be polite, but the booking agent would have to find her another band. Thirty seconds later, she realized that wouldn't be necessary.

With the sustained sound of the flute hanging in the air, Brodie suddenly ripped into the drums, pounding out a vibrant beat. Lancer came in with an undercurrent of throbbing bass. Piper moved with the rousing rhythms, completely engaged as the sultry sound of Karen's contralto voice mingled with Daniel's dynamic chords.

Relieved because she wouldn't have to reject the band after all, Piper finished her soda and set

down the glass. She didn't want the group's disappointment or anything else to spoil the joy
brought on by her sudden realization of the
obvious: She didn't have to let small problems
ruin her life. Swaying in her chair, she lost herself in the music and the moment.

The song ended when the four musicians
stopped playing in precise, abrupt unison.
Before Piper had adjusted to the sudden silence,
the group eased into a slow, sensual ballad that
would bring potential couples closer together on
the dance floor. They ended with a fast song that
had just recently hit the charts. Without a doubt,
With a Vengeance was a keeper.

"Yes!" Piper applauded with unbridled
enthusiasm.

"That means you love us, right?" Daniel
asked with an exaggerated, quizzical expression.

Piper burst out laughing. "You're great!"

"So when do we start?" Karen jumped off the
stage and placed the flute in the velvet-lined
case lying open on a nearby table. Given the
careful way the young woman handled the
instrument, Piper assumed it was among her
most prized possessions.

"Yesterday would have been good," the dour
bass player said. "My stomach is grumbling a
second bass line."

"You're hungry? Are you that broke?" Piper
spoke without thinking and covered her mouth to
stifle another laugh. Although Lancer had used

humor to make a point, she didn't want the band to think she was amused by their dire financial situation. She coughed to quell her giggles when she noticed that Karen was watching her intently.

"We could use the job," Daniel said.

"We need the exposure," Karen quickly added. "Mason said that P3 is one of the most popular dance clubs in the city."

Pleased, Piper glanced around the warehouse basement she had transformed into a favorite hangout for San Francisco's discerning singles. "We're packed every night we have live music."

Daniel poked his arm. "Yep, I'm live."

"And hired." Piper picked up her soda and took a long swallow to wash down another bout of chuckles. Apparently, now that she had decided to lighten up, she had opened a floodgate of suppressed mirth.

"We start Thursday, then?" Karen asked.

Piper nodded. "Nine to one, Thursday through Saturday."

"Excellent!" Brodie tossed a drumstick in the air and caught it behind his back.

"I'll tell Mason to write up the contract." Karen snapped the flute case closed and tucked it under her arm. "Would you mind if we set up Wednesday afternoon and have a short practice session?"

Piper agreed without hesitation. "Anytime after two. My security system is state of the art if you want to leave your gear."

A horn honked in the alley.

"Just push everything behind the backdrop." Piper waved toward the curtains at the back of the stage and set her glass on the bar. "I'll be out back if you need me."

Piper's buoyant mood persisted as she headed toward the back door. Since Leo had been delayed, she wasn't even upset that the delivery truck was later than promised. She smiled as she pictured her desperate husband trying to stem the flow of toilet water before the upstairs of the old Victorian mansion was awash. He knew that, left unattended, a flood would have caused expensive repairs and more stress, neither of which her overwrought nerves could stand.

When Leo popped out of the storeroom door, Piper gasped and clutched her chest. "I said no dramatic entrances!"

"But I just—" Leo frowned, puzzled, and then snapped a horrified glance toward the storage room. "Is somebody in there?"

"No." Piper shook her head and giggled.

"What's funny?" Leo asked, looking more confused.

"Uh—I'm not sure." Piper held out her hands, palms up, and shrugged. "Guess I'm just feeling good because I decided to take Paige's advice. I do worry too much about everything."

"I can't argue with that." Leo relaxed, grinning.

"No more, though." Piper covered her mouth, but she couldn't silence her laughter. "Sorry, but the new bass player had me cracking up."

"It's hard to imagine someone from a group called With a Vengeance being funny," Leo said.

Piper mimicked Lancer's pathetic tone as she unlocked the rear doors. "'My stomach's grumbling a second bass line.'"

Leo blinked. "I don't get it."

Piper was still giggling so hard, she had trouble trying to explain. "Stomach grumbling . . . like a bass sound?"

Leo shrugged.

"Think about it." Piper threw open the back doors.

"I understand the joke," Leo said as the truck driver handed Piper an invoice. "I just don't think it's that funny."

"That's okay, dear." Piper smiled.

Paige locked the trunk of her lime green VW Bug and pocketed the keys. Her purse was safer in the car than anywhere in the Fifth Street Shelter, an old building on the edge of the harbor warehouse district.

As long as no one takes the car, Paige thought as she hurried across the gravel parking area.

Doug Wilson joked that sooner or later one of the shelter's destitute regulars would steal the small safe in his storeroom office. As a precaution against the inevitable, he didn't keep anything valuable in it.

"You're late," Doug barked in a gravelly voice when the door slammed behind Paige. He shook pepper into a huge pot of beef stew.

"By two minutes!" Paige glanced at the wall clock above the massive stove. It was just past five thirty. "I had some last-minute stuff to finish on Stanley's application for Hawthorn Hill."

"Excuses, excuses." Doug wiped his hands on a white apron stained with various unidentified sauces. He glanced back with a surly scowl. "Can't depend on anyone anymore."

In his late forties with a lean, wiry build, the shelter supervisor was not nearly as unappreciative or as tough as he looked. He couldn't hide the caring reflected in his gray-green eyes, and he wore the bristle of a beard as a badge of defiance. Rumor had it that he had once been a high-tech computer guru. Doug wouldn't talk about his past, except to say that he was unemployable because he only shaved when he felt like it.

"So did the application get sent?" Doug asked, trying to sound casual.

"It went out in the five o'clock mail." Paige grabbed another clean but stained apron off a hook and slipped it on. "Is Stanley here, yet?"

"No, but Kevin Graves is." Doug waved a spoon toward the serving counter that separated the kitchen from the dining area.

A young man sat on a stool at the far end of the counter stuffing paper napkins into metal holders.

"So that's the new guy, huh?" Paige asked, trying not to sound too interested. With short blond hair, blue eyes, a perfect profile, and a killer tan, Kevin Graves was handsome in a classic Californian way. *Not the usual volunteer type*, Paige noted, intrigued.

"That's him," Doug said.

"What's his story?" Paige asked. "Did the beach police revoke his surfing privileges?"

"No." Doug dropped a lid on the stew pot and cast her a wry look. "He was injured in a construction accident, and it left him with a permanent limp. Until he finds another line of work, he wants to do something constructive with his time."

"Oh." Blushing, Paige glanced back at the young man and noticed the wooden cane hooked on the counter beside him. For a witch on the demonic world's most wanted list, her powers of observation left a lot to be desired. "Do I look as ridiculous as I feel with my foot in my mouth?"

"I don't think anyone else will notice." Doug turned when the door opened again and a middle-aged woman entered. "Hey, Ms. Ryan! Glad to see you."

Wearing designer jeans, a stylish sweater, and leather boots that probably cost more than Paige

made in a week, Jennifer Ryan smiled with gen-
uine warmth when Doug introduced her to
Paige.

"Paige has worked here before, which makes
her an expert on our dinner routine." Doug
grabbed a scorched pot holder, opened the oven,
and removed a large tin of hot rolls. "She'll show
you what to do."

Taking the hint, Paige handed Jennifer an
apron and waved her to follow. "The routine is
pretty basic. We scoop whatever Doug cooks
onto plates. Most nights we only have one main
dish, so the line usually moves right along."

"I think I can handle that," Jennifer said.

Unlike some of the rich contributors Paige
dealt with at the clinic, there was no trace of superiority in Jennifer Ryan's attitude. It was, Paige
decided, entirely possible that the woman had
been motivated to donate her time by an honest
desire to give something back to the community.

"We also stock the dish bins and fill the
condiments before the meal," Paige continued,
"and we help clean up afterward."

When they reached the counter, Kevin
unhooked his cane and slid off the stool. "I'm
happy to report that the silverware bins and the
napkin holders are full," he said, saluting with
his free hand and grinning.

"You've been busy." Smiling back, Paige
started to hold out her hand. She pulled back
when she realized that Kevin had his right hand

on the cane to support himself. She quickly tried to smooth over the awkward moment. "This is Jennifer, and I'm Paige."

"I'm delighted." If Kevin noticed her discomfort, he didn't show it. "You certainly live up to everything I've heard about you."

"What exactly did you hear?" Paige asked with wary curiosity. Was the space between her and Kevin really supercharged with mutual interest, or was she imagining the chemistry? She rarely felt an instant attraction to anyone, and the effect was disconcerting.

"That you were a beautiful angel," Kevin said, "full of goodness and light."

"Doug said that?" Paige asked, stunned. The gruff boss of the Fifth Street Shelter disdained poetry and sissy words. Had he seen her orb somewhere without her knowing it?

"No, some old guy did. When he asked if you were here and I told him you weren't, he shuffled off toward the rest room, talking to himself." Kevin nodded toward the far end of the dining hall. "I couldn't help but overhear."

"Stanley Addison," Paige said, relieved. She doubted that the old man had seen her orb, but even if he had, it wouldn't be too serious. No one paid any attention or gave any credence to the nonsensical ramblings of the senile senior.

"Someone special?" Jennifer asked.

Paige nodded, realizing the affection she felt for the old man was evident on her face. "He's a sweet, totally harmless, slightly addled old man with no family—at least none that we can find. Since he collects Social Security, I'm trying to get him into the Hawthorn Hill Home for low-income retired people."

"So you really are an angel, then," Jennifer said.

"Mr. Addison's angel anyway," Kevin added. "Maybe he isn't so addled after all."

"It's my job to help people," Paige explained, embarrassed. The intensity of Kevin's blue-eyed gaze seemed to set her blood on fire. She rubbed the crimson flush creeping up her neck.

"Okay, you guys!" Doug called out. "Social hour's over. The hungry horde will be storming through the door any minute, so let's get to work!"

Doug to the rescue! Paige thought with silent gratitude. She needed a break from the tension.

Jennifer glanced at Doug. "The taskmaster with a heart of gold, right?"

"Yeah," Paige agreed, "but most of the time he forgets that we're not paid employees, which may explain why this shelter has a huge volunteer turnover."

Jennifer shrugged. "I think he's cute."

"A diamond in the rough." Paige stole a glance at the older woman's left hand. No wedding ring. The week was certainly getting off to an interesting start.

The next three hours whizzed by as Paige,

Doug, and the new recruits served dinner to thirty-five hungry men and women who lived on the street for thirty-five different reasons. Some of them preferred to fend for themselves on the outside at night. Others slept at the shelter. Tonight, setting up the cots had been delayed while Doug walked Jennifer to her car.

"So are we done?" Kevin held on to the prep table with one hand and hung a large serving spoon on a nail in the wall above it.

"That's it." Paige tossed her apron into a laundry bag.

Kevin turned and leaned against the table to brace himself. "Are you going straight home?"

Paige hesitated, anticipating Kevin's next question. Although his interest was obvious to anyone with eyes and a rudimentary command of the language—body and English—it hadn't occurred to her that he might ask her out so soon. If he did, she wasn't sure if she wanted to go. Not without getting to know him a little better. She decided to fudge for time. "I want to make sure Stanley's settled in for the night before I leave," Paige said.

"Stanley just left." Kevin glanced toward the front door.

Paige threw up her hands. After much argument, she had finally convinced Doug to keep a sleeping spot available for Stanley Addison. However, the old guy sometimes forgot the shelter's routine and wandered out. He almost always returned before Doug locked up for the night.

"He'll be back," Paige said. "I hope."

"You're going to wait?" Kevin asked.

"At least until I'm sure that Doug won't lock him out. I'm this close to getting Stanley admitted to Hawthorn Hill." Paige held her thumb and forefinger an inch apart to illustrate. "I'd feel awful if he had an accident on the street before I closed the deal."

"You really like the old guy, don't you?" Kevin sounded pleased, as though he understood the need to help others that motivated her.

Actually, Paige realized, *since Kevin volunteered to work, he might be as of much a do-gooder as I am.* The combination of good looks and a good heart was hard to resist.

"I adore Stanley," Paige said. "Everything will probably work out for him, which is great, but"—she paused, sighing—"there are just so many people in trouble, and way too often they've been hurt by circumstances beyond their control. I wish I could help them all, but I can't. It's just not possible."

"But you care," Kevin said. "That's more than a lot of people can say."

"Maybe, but sometimes the hopelessness of it all just wears me out." Paige paused, unable to explain that her experiences with unspeakable, supernatural evil added to the burden of mortal misery. Although Kevin was sympathetic, the detour into hopeless despair had to be a turnoff.

"I think you're being way too hard on yourself." Kevin reached for his cane, which was hanging on the end of the table. He could stand unassisted for short periods of time and had alternately stood or sat on a stool while he helped serve dinner. The cane provided support when he walked.

"Your cane is beautiful. Is it an antique?" Paige asked with an admiring glance at the staff. The curved, silver handle was engraved with fine, swirling lines that continued unbroken into the upper portion of the polished wooden shaft. Great care and pride had gone into the craftsmanship.

"As a matter of fact, it is. Family heirloom." Kevin raised the cane so Paige could examine it more closely. The movement unbalanced him, and he staggered sideways.

"Careful!" As Paige reached out to steady him, the straight end of the wooden cane flipped up and hit her arm. Startled by a small, static shock, she recoiled slightly.

Oblivious to the hazards of his flyaway cane, Kevin caught the edge of the table, pulled himself upright, and planted the cane on the floor. "Sorry. I'm not usually such a klutz."

"No problem—" Paige swayed, suddenly dizzy.

"Are you all right?" Kevin gripped Paige's arm with his free hand. "You look a little pale."

"I'm fine." Suddenly overcome with exhaustion, Paige clamped onto the table to keep her legs from buckling.

"Why am I not convinced?" Kevin frowned. "Maybe you caught some weird bug one of these people dragged in from the street. They don't live in the most sanitary conditions."

Paige waved off his concern. "I'm just tired. Between my regular job and working here last week, I didn't get as much rest as I probably needed."

Paige didn't add that she had spent most of the weekend working with Piper to improve her memory skills. According to Leo, failure to recall an incantation or other pertinent magical lore had brought about the premature demise of many a good witch. She did not intend to join the ranks of the forgetful dead.

Paige tightened her grip on the table when another wave of dizziness washed over her. "Maybe I'd better sit down for a few minutes."

"Maybe you'd better let me drive you home," Kevin suggested as Paige settled onto a stool.

Paige started to protest, then realized her options were limited. If she tried to drive, she might pass out from fatigue. Piper was working at P3, and Phoebe was still in class. Leo would orb in if she called, but since the nearest bus stop was several blocks away, she didn't want to explain how he had arrived without wheels on such short notice.

"I'd love a ride, Kevin, if you're sure it's not too much trouble."

"No trouble at all." Kevin grinned. "What about your car?"

"My brother-in-law can pick it up later, after P3 closes," Paige said, yawning.

Phoebe felt overwhelmed by the amount of information the community college instructor had dumped on the class. She and twenty-four other students had been introduced to several basic Web site construction functions, most of which involved complex command sequences they were expected to have memorized by the following Monday.

"I love messing around with computers," the young woman sitting beside Phoebe said, "but so far, this course is completely boring."

"My head is spinning," Phoebe said with a glance at Kate Dustin. Peaches-and-cream pretty, with blue eyes and a bright smile, Kate was the only other student in the class who had reached the ripe old age of twenty-five.

"Not that Mr. Deekle cares," Phoebe added. "I am absolutely positive he was born without a funny bone."

At the front of the room, a tall, gangling man with a mustache as sparse as his thinning hair shut down his computer. Wayne Deekle's bearing was as stiff as his monotonous delivery. He had not cracked a smile the whole night. If

Phoebe managed to master the art of Web site design, it would be in spite of the instructor's lifeless lectures.

"Ha!" Kate choked back a laugh and waved Phoebe into the hall. "I was under the impression that twenty-first-century computer geeks were all brainy hunks. Silly me."

"Mr. Deekle is stuck in the *last* century," Phoebe said. They left the building through double swinging doors behind three young men walking a few yards ahead. They were all good-looking athletic types with smarts. *A cluster of potential corporate success*, she thought with a nod toward the group. "Those Web master wanna-bes taking the class with us are the new millennium models."

"You could be right about that." Sighing, Kate focused on the three men as they hurried across the parking lot. When they went into Compute-A-Cup across the street, she looked at Phoebe with a sly grin. "Want to join me for a cup of coffee?"

The invitation caught Phoebe off guard. She hadn't socialized much with the younger, college crowd while she had been an undergraduate at the university. Aside from the age gap, the witch thing made it difficult to form solid friendships.

Kate was close to her in age, though, and just wanted female cover while she trolled for male company. Phoebe had no desire to fend off eager campus studs, but she welcomed the chance to relax after the grueling class. Cole was out of town, Paige was working at the shelter, and Piper and Leo would be at P3 until the wee hours. She didn't have to rush home.

"Coffee sounds great," Phoebe said, "but I can't stay too long. I have to go home and review my notes before I forget what they mean."

"I can so relate." Kate entered the quaint café and nodded with approval as she glanced around. "Cool place, huh?"

Phoebe had to agree. Baskets of live plants hung from the ceiling. The walls were covered with prints of famous paintings, bulletin boards full of notes and flyers advertising everything from upcoming concerts to yard sales, and racks of books, magazines, and newspapers. Furnished with mismatched tables, chairs, and upholstered sofas, Compute-A-Cup was busy without being jammed packed and seemed to attract a quiet, studious clientele.

Maybe because every table is equipped with a computer and Internet access, Phoebe thought. One of the men they had followed inside turned on his table computer before he finished sitting down.

"Let's sit over there." Kate pointed to a corner table on the opposite side of the room from their male classmates. She jumped to grab it before someone else staked a claim.

Phoebe joined her as a man perched on a stool with a twelve-string guitar began to sing an Irish ballad. Kate's company, a hot cappuccino, and the folksinger's mellow tenor were just what she needed to take the edge off another long day of being unemployed.

"Thanks so much for coming with me," Kate said as Phoebe sat down and dropped her books on the floor. She pushed the flat computer screen against the wall without turning it on.

"Thanks for asking me." Phoebe leaned back when a student waitress arrived to wipe crumbs off the table.

"Do you guys know what you want?" The girl waited expectantly, pen poised over her order pad.

"Mocha cappuccino and cheesecake with strawberries, if you have it." As long as she was hanging out college style, Phoebe thought, she might as well indulge her sweet tooth. She could work off the extra calories in the Manor's basement gym tomorrow.

"We got it." The waitress looked at Kate, who ordered the same.

After the girl left, Kate's gaze flicked toward the three men huddled around their computer screens. "I really do appreciate it, Phoebe. I like to unwind after intense brain work, but I would have felt funny sitting here alone."

"No problem," Phoebe said honestly. "Except for studying, I didn't have anything better to do."

"What? No man in your life?" Kate's eyes widened with disbelief.

Phoebe didn't want to discuss her personal life with a stranger. Her gaze fell on Kate's wide gold bracelet, which was engraved with an intricate, Celtic braid design. "What an unusual piece," she said to change the subject.

"It belonged to my great-grandmother"—Kate paused, frowning thoughtfully—"or maybe it was my great-great-grandmother. Whatever. There's writing etched inside, but I've never been able to make it out." She slipped the bracelet off and pressed it into Phoebe's hand. "Maybe you can."

Phoebe's response fizzled into a guttural grunt as a vision flooded her mind.

. . . *Kate, wearing crude metal armor over fur and leather, stood by a huge tree. Lightning arrowed downward from a rip in the black clouds that streaked the sky. The bolt hit the base of a towering tree, felling the timber in a cascade of exploding sparks.* . . .

Phoebe dropped the bracelet as she snapped out of the trance. Although the vision left her stomach in knots, she quickly regained her outward composure. Thankfully, Kate was watching the folksinger and seemed unaware of the brief lapse.

"Anything?" Kate asked, turning back to Phoebe.

"What do you mean?" Phoebe asked, her tone wary.

"The inscription." Kate put the bracelet back on. "Guess you couldn't figure out what it says either."

Phoebe shook her head, relieved her trance state had not been noticed, but feeling queasy. Based on the barbaric wardrobe and surroundings, she was certain the violent images were from Kate's past, not her future. Since she couldn't change the woman's history, there was no point bringing up the disturbing event until the Charmed connection became apparent.

"Here we go." A waitress appeared carrying two large cups of cappuccino and two plates of New York–style cheesecake topped with a strawberry sauce.

Phoebe blinked when the girl set a mug and plate in front of her. "Did I order cheesecake?"

Chapter

3

"That's none of your business, Doug." Paige scowled at the phone. She usually shrugged off Doug's teasing, but today she was too tired and irritable to tolerate his impudence.

"I think it's great that you and Kevin hit it off, Paige," Doug said. "You're too young to spend so much of your free time serving squashed spuds to a bunch of street people."

"I thought you liked street people." Paige saw her boss staring from across the room. She had been twenty minutes late to work because she had overslept. One of the few things Mr. Cowan disliked more than a habitually tardy employee was an employee who used clinic time and phones for personal business. Her record in that department wasn't exemplary, either.

"It's okay for *me* to hang with the homeless," Doug said, his tone serious. "I'm a cranky, burned-out has-been."

"Jennifer didn't seem to mind," Paige countered.

Doug ignored the reference to his new fan club of one. "Did you call for a reason?"

"Yeah," Paige said. "I just wanted to know if Stanley showed up last night." She covered her mouth to hide a yawn, then smiled tightly at Mr. Cowan. He frowned and went into his office.

"Stanley came in around eleven, snored all night, and left at eight." Doug sighed. "Any word from Hawthorn Hill?"

"I just sent Stanley's application yesterday, Doug." Paige understood the shelter supervisor's frustration. He had worked in, with, and around the system for years, and sometimes it felt like the wheels of bureaucracy didn't turn at all. "I'm hoping to get word by the end of the week, next Monday at the latest."

"Right, and just in case you're wondering"— Doug hesitated as though to emphasize the point—"Kevin's working here all week."

Paige hung up, but she could imagine Doug laughing. Annoyed, she pushed a potted cactus toward the corner of her desk and flipped open Stanley's file to update her notes. Although Doug probably wouldn't believe it, the only spot Kevin Graves had in her future was standing beside her on the shelter food line.

The ride home last night had been totally uneventful. She and Kevin had talked about her work at the clinic, the construction accident that shattered his leg, the shelter, and Stanley. There had been no awkward, lingering moment of hoping to prolong the conversation as she had gotten out of his older, fuel-efficient, sensible car. Just a quick "good-bye, thanks, see-you-tomorrow," and Kevin had driven away.

Paige frowned, puzzled. She didn't think she had imagined the intense chemistry between her and Kevin, and she felt positive he had sensed it too. So what happened to dampen the attraction? The fact that she kept dozing off between sentences on the ride home probably hadn't helped. What if Kevin thought he bored her? That would certainly explain his sudden lack of interest.

"Not scintillating soap opera material, that's for sure," Paige mumbled.

"Did you say something?" Lila paused by Paige's desk.

"Nothing important." Paige was deliberately evasive. Until she figured out what was going on with Kevin, she didn't want to be pressured for daily progress reports from her curious, well-meaning coworker.

"Okay." Lila snagged her sweater on the spines of Paige's new cactus as she turned to leave. She didn't notice and kept walking.

Paige winced as the micro-disaster unfolded.

Her first thought was that the slow-growing plant might be irrevocably damaged in the fall.

Secondly, since Mr. Cowan occasionally complained about the cards, candles, and other knickknacks in her cubicle, she didn't want to call his attention to her expanding collection.

When Lila's sweater pulled the pot off the desk, Paige instinctively tried to save it.

"Plant," Paige hissed, expecting the endangered cactus to orb unharmed into her hands.

Instead the small pot hit the floor and broke apart. Then shards of terra-cotta, a pile of dirt, and the uprooted plant vanished from the floor in a swirl of light and materialized in her hands.

Paige clamped her hands together to keep loose soil from falling between her fingers onto the floor. A cactus spine pricked her palm. She dropped the whole mess as Lila looked back.

"What happened?" Lila asked.

That's what Paige wanted to know. What *had* just happened?

"Don't worry about it, Lila. I'm sure the cactus will survive." *I'll worry instead,* Paige thought as she bent over and carefully picked up the plant. Bits of dirt and chipped clay pot were stuck on and around the sharp needles. She had been working a lot and not sleeping enough lately, but Piper and Phoebe had never warned her that fatigue might affect her powers.

Paige forced her heavy eyelids open as she

scooped dirt into her coffee mug and placed the cactus in its temporary home. Maybe taking a nap would cure orb delay.

"You haven't said much about your Web site class." Piper rinsed a peeled potato and glanced over her shoulder as she dropped it into a pot on the stove.

Phoebe looked up from the laptop on the table. "It's too soon to tell if I'm wasting my time or not."

Actually, that's only partially correct, Phoebe thought. She hadn't said anything because the whole evening was a blur. She didn't remember much except that the instructor was boring and she had enjoyed talking to Kate Dustin at Compute-A-Cup afterward. She didn't recall the details of the conversation, but then she wasn't angling for dates or obsessing over the latest fashion fads. Fortunately she had taken copious notes in class or she'd be completely lost in the next session tomorrow night.

"But you've always been the technical brains in this outfit," Piper said.

"Yeah, well, driving around a neighborhood is a lot easier than building a house." Phoebe sighed. "The same goes for cruising the Web and constructing sites. Cruising is a snap."

Phoebe stared at the text displayed on the computer screen. She had no trouble creating a link to another Web site when the instructions were in front of her, but she couldn't seem to commit the simple exercise to memory.

"I bet building a Web site is a lot easier than building a house, and cheaper, too." Piper chuckled softly as she stuffed the potato peels into the garbage disposal. She turned on the water to fill the receptacle, inserted the black stopper in the drain, and flipped the disposal switch.

When Piper shrieked, Phoebe's heart lurched. She looked up as the plastic drain stopper shot into the air on a geyser of mutilated vegetable skins.

Piper burst out laughing.

"Hit the switch!" Phoebe slammed her laptop closed to protect it from spraying potato peel mash.

"Got it!" Piper shut down the disposal, but the fountain of ground garbage and water didn't stop.

Saving the laptop was Phoebe's only priority. With the device clutched to her chest, she started toward the hall and barely escaped being clobbered when Leo threw open the basement door.

"What's the matter?" Leo asked, breathless from racing up the stairs. For room-to-room emergencies, running was sometimes quicker than orbing.

Piper was laughing too hard to talk. She waved at the gushing fountain in the sink and turned off the tap. The water plume subsided, but resumed at full force within seconds.

"We seem to have a major malfunction in the garbage disposal." Phoebe shoved the laptop into a drawer.

"It won't shut off," Piper sputtered. She reached for a dish towel to wipe her splattered face, realized that the towel was dripping watery potato gunk, and tossed it over her shoulder in frustration. She caught her lip in her teeth, but she couldn't stifle her giggles.

Standing outside the spray radius, Phoebe smiled too. It would take hours to clean up the starchy glop that clung to everything within several feet of the sink, including Piper, but at least her older sister was seeing the humor in the situation and not freaking out.

"Maybe it's a broken pipe." Leo took a step toward the sink and slipped on the potato slime coating the floor.

"Careful!" Phoebe winced as he grabbed the counter to stop his fall.

A huge guffaw escaped Piper before she clamped a hand over her mouth. "Sorry, Leo."

"That's okay. If a little slapstick keeps you laughing, I'm happy to oblige." Smiling, Leo opened the cabinet door and stuck his head inside. When he backed out, his expression was grave. "It's not a broken pipe."

"But that's good, isn't it?" Phoebe asked, puzzled by his sudden change in demeanor.

"That depends." Leo turned a valve to shut off the water to the faucet, closed the cabinet door, and stood up. He ran his finger around the wet drain and held it out for Piper and Phoebe to see. A roughly circular, paper-thin, shiny green disk half an inch in diameter stuck to his skin.

"What's that?" Piper asked.

"Bad news," Leo said.

Phoebe frowned. The upstairs toilet had over-flowed yesterday, and now the garbage disposal had run amok. Neither event endangered life or limb, but they probably weren't a coincidence, either. "Bad like in some kind of sludge demon with a warped sense of evil?"

"Bad like in gremlin," Leo said. "They're like underworld rats, only uglier, nastier, and smarter. A lot of them are immune to magic, but they *all* shed scales." He flicked the green grem-lin scale into the trash can under the sink.

"Then how do we get rid of it?" Piper leaned over the sink to peer down the drain.

"Trap it and turn it loose in its natural habi-tat." Leo glanced at the floor. "Down there."

"Is there some kind of no-kill taboo on grem-lins?" Phoebe asked.

"No," Leo said, "but when a gremlin dies, others sense it and move in to fill the vacated niche. The only way to break the cycle is to catch the first squatter. When a gremlin is trapped or forced out, it releases a warning pheromone. We can't detect it, but the scent repulses other grem-lins and breaks the species's territorial bond."

"Figures. There's not even an easy way to vanquish evil vermin." Now that the rubbish rain had stopped, Phoebe moved closer to the counter. "See anything, Piper?"

Still bent over the sink, Piper shook her head. "No, but it's dark down—"

The cabinet door burst open, and a screeching, slimy green creature that resembled a foot-tall frog with teeth bolted between Leo's legs.

"Look out!" Piper's warning rode another wave of surprised laughter.

As the mini–swamp thing charged, Phoebe's levitating power engaged. However, instead of *rocketing* toward the ceiling to evade the unexpected assault, she *floated* upward. The critter slashed at her boot with glistening fangs as it barreled by, leaving teeth marks in the leather.

Piper coughed to silence a chuckle and asked, "Was that a gremlin?"

Leo nodded. "I'm afraid so."

Phoebe settled back to the floor with more than an evil rat-frog and a scarred boot weighing on her mind. Why had she drifted out of danger when zooming to safety would have been a more appropriate response?

In her psychology courses, Phoebe had learned that stress often caused physical and mental aberrations, which might account for the weakened flight response and her sudden inability to retain a few, simple facts. Was she suppressing anxiety about Cole's physical and emotional absences without being aware of it? Would that affect her ability to function?

Or was she allergic to gremlins?

Either way, Phoebe thought, *I'd better figure it out and snap out of it soon.* For safety's sake, she couldn't afford to have her brain and her magic misfiring.

Phoebe didn't want to alarm Leo and Piper unnecessarily, but all magical glitches were cause for concern. "I think we might have a problem."

"I know we do. How much trouble is this little green gremlin gonna be, Leo?" Piper was no longer amused. "On a scale of one to ten."

"One, if we're talking about life-threatening evil," Leo explained. "There are different classifications of gremlins, but this one looks like the common household variety. It's not particularly dangerous, but it rates a ten for annoying and destructive."

"In other words, expensive." Piper sighed.

"What's it doing here, though?" As she posed the question, Phoebe had the uneasy feeling she had forgotten something important.

"Running loose in the house." Piper cocked an eyebrow at Leo, as though it were his fault.

Leo glanced toward the hall. "Actually, it'll probably head for the nearest way back into the plumbing."

"I meant why did it decide to infest *our* house," Phoebe clarified.

"Because the Manor is full of magic and old pipes." Leo closed the basement door. "Both of which would attract a displaced plumbing gremlin."

"You mean it's lost?" Phoebe blinked.

"It was until we found it," Piper quipped. "Now we just have to—"

"Freeze it!" Phoebe yelled as the critter raced back into the kitchen and leaped into the sink.

Piper's hands shot out as the grotesque beastie stuck its head in the drain. "Gotcha!"

Phoebe wrinkled her nose as she studied the creature in the sink. A mottled, greenish brown body was immobilized in an upended position with two powerful hind legs splayed. Webbed, amphibian feet were armed with hooked, retractable claws. The front legs and feet were smaller versions of the back pair, just like a frog or terrestrial toad. *Toads*, Phoebe noted, *are cuddly cute by comparison.*

"That's a lucky break," Leo said. "It looks like magic works on this one."

"Look again." Piper pointed. The double-jointed critter began to ooze into the pipes as the effects of her power wore off.

Leo grabbed the gremlin's foot, but he couldn't hold on to the slippery appendage.

Phoebe shuddered as the fanged frog vanished into the plumbing. "Okay. That was fun, but you guys are on your own for the hunt-and-trap phase of this operation."

"Can't handle the slime, huh?" Leo teased.

"No, I have to study for my class tomorrow night." Phoebe grimaced as she glanced around the kitchen, which was covered with potato paste. "In the living room."

"Yeah, it is kind of messy in here." Piper wiped a smear off her nose. "Go study. Leo and I will clean up."

"Thanks." Phoebe turned toward the table and paused. "What happened to my laptop?"

"It's in the hutch, where you just put it." Leo reached under the sink to turn the water back on. "Middle drawer."

"Oh, right." Phoebe retrieved the computer and made a quick exit before Leo or Piper questioned the lapse of memory.

Piper paused outside the attic door, her arms loaded with clothes sealed in plastic bags. She was tired of jamming his and her wardrobes into one small bedroom closet and had finally packed several outfits she hadn't worn for months. Since she wasn't sure she wanted to part with the chic but outdated fashions, she had decided to store them in the attic. One of these days she and her sisters might actually agree to sort through generations of accumulated Halliwell stuff and have a gigantic yard sale.

"But probably not," Piper muttered as she braced the stack of clothes against the wall and reached for the doorknob. When she saw that the door was unlatched, she kicked it open and hurried inside. She dropped the pile of clothes in the nearest unoccupied space and turned to see Paige rummaging through one of Grams's old trunks.

"Hey, Paige. What are you doing?"

"Looking for this." Paige held up a small ceramic bowl painted with a delicate floral design. "It's perfect."

"It belonged to Grams," Piper said, her tone crisp. "She kept pins in it."

"Jewelry pins?" Paige asked, yawning.

"Straight pins for sewing, diaper pins, safety pins, hat pins—you name it." Piper walked over and flopped down on a pile of pillows. "No matter what kind of pin we needed, we knew right where to find it."

"Then this is even more perfect." Smiling, Paige closed the trunk. She settled back on her heels and sagged slightly, still holding the fragile bowl. "Something that Grams used, I mean."

"Perfect for what?" Piper leaned forward, anticipating a fumble when Paige's eyelids began to droop. It was only nine o'clock, but the double-duty schedule of working all day at South Bay Social Services and the early evening hours at the Fifth Street Shelter was obviously wearing her down.

Paige jerked her head up, but her hands and the bowl dropped into her lap. "A cactus plant at work. The little spiny dude needs a new pot so I can have my coffee mug back."

"Uh-huh." Piper started to protest, then hesitated. Like her, Phoebe would be upset if something happened to the antique bowl, but she couldn't say no. Paige could have bought a cactus pot for a couple bucks. Instead she had deliberately looked for something with a family connection. Grams's pin bowl was just another means of bridging the years Paige had been excluded from the Halliwell family history.

"What happened to the old pot?" Piper asked.

Before Paige could answer, Phoebe burst through the attic door. Her frantic gaze focused on *The Book of Shadows*.

Startled by Phoebe's abrupt entrance, Paige shifted position. The bowl rolled off her lap. She extended her hand to orb it just as Piper raised her hands to freeze.

"Bowl!" Paige commanded.

Piper tensed as the irreplaceable heirloom froze for an instant, then continued its forward roll. It landed, unbroken, on the worn carpet.

"*That's* what happened," Paige said in answer to Piper's question about the old pot.

"*Nothing* happened." Piper frowned when the bowl suddenly orbed into Paige's hand.

"Exactly." Pale and shaken, Paige cradled the bowl against her stomach.

Piper stared at her own hands.

"Did someone call a meeting?" Phoebe paused, looking confused as she cast a sweeping glance around the attic.

"No," Piper said. "We just all had stuff to do up here."

"Bowl." Paige held up the pin bowl, which was firmly clasped in two hands.

"Pack and store." Piper pointed at the pile of plastic clothes bags and looked at Phoebe expectantly. "You?"

Phoebe blinked. "Not a clue."

"Meaning what?" Piper had to cover her mouth to keep from laughing aloud at her sister's perplexed expression. Her freeze power had just failed, which wasn't even remotely funny, but she couldn't seem to muzzle her glee. What was up with that?

Phoebe turned her palms up and shrugged. "I don't *remember* why I came up here."

"Don't you hate that?" Paige rolled her eyes and yawned again. "Happens to me all the time. I'll go into the kitchen to get something and draw a total blank."

"And then remember what it was you wanted right after you leave," Piper added. "Or you put something somewhere and can't find it two minutes later. That happens to me all the time too."

Smiling tightly, Phoebe sank into the old rocker beside Paige. "Me too, but this is different. I've had a couple *dozen* short-term memory lapses today, and that's *never* happened to me before."

Paige's brow creased in a thoughtful frown. "I've never had orb delay before, either."

"Is that what just happened with the bowl?" Piper asked, muffling another chuckle. "A delayed reaction?"

"I don't know what else to call it." Paige scowled at Piper, annoyed. "It's not funny."

"I know, I just"—Piper was at a loss to explain—"everything just seems funny to me."

"That's weird," Phoebe said.

"Should we be worried?" Paige asked.

"Yes, but I'm not sure about what." Piper snapped her head around when Leo walked in carrying a large adjustable pipe wrench. He had spent the past several hours plotting how to snare their uninvited gremlin guest. "Did you catch it?"

"Not yet, but I will." The set of Leo's jaw, his hardened gaze, and demeanor reflected an intense determination. "I have to shut down the pipe valves to the radiator up here. If I limit where the gremlin can go, I'll improve my chances and save time."

"Gremlin?" Phoebe's eyes widened. "What gremlin?"

Paige looked at Piper askance.

"Show, don't tell," Piper suggested.

Nodding, Paige held out her hand. "Wrench!"

Expecting the wrench to turn into sparkling light in his hand, Leo let go.

As the heavy tool dropped, Piper whipped out her hands. She muttered softly, "Come on . . ."

The wrench froze for a split second, then hit the floor and orbed into Paige's hand.

"What was that all about?" Leo looked stunned.

"Slow orb, short freeze, and memory loss," Piper said. "When the gremlin wiggled out of my freeze this afternoon, I thought it was immune to magic, like you said. Apparently that's not the problem. *My* power is fizzling out."

"Apparently mine is too," Paige said. "I've been so tired all day; I thought that's why my orb was off."

"Can gremlins drain powers?" Piper asked.

"Not that I've heard of." Leo ran his hand over his hair and rubbed his neck as he paced. He glanced at Phoebe. "Are you having problems with your powers?"

"I'm not sure." Phoebe cupped her chin in her hand, her eyes narrowed. "I don't remember having any visions lately, but that doesn't mean I *didn't* have one. Maybe I forgot." She looked up. "Did I fly today?"

"Yes!" Piper grinned. "You levitated so the gremlin wouldn't run into you, but very slowly."

"Slowly?" Phoebe rocked forward, planted her feet, and clasped her hands on her knees. "Under those circumstances, shouldn't I have *shot* into the air?"

"Now that you mention it, yes." Leo dropped into a squat between Piper and Paige. "So something *has* diminished all your powers."

"But nothing strange happened to me today—or yesterday, or the day before." Piper paused, thinking back over recent events. The sudden appearance of the gremlin was the only supernatural anomaly in an unbelievably routine week.

"Not unless getting your sense of humor back counts," Paige observed. She braced her elbow on the old trunk and rested her head in her hand. Her eyes fluttered closed.

"You *have* been laughing a lot lately, Piper." Leo straightened suddenly.

"Do you think it's indicative of a bigger problem?" Phoebe's face darkened. "My short-term memory isn't working right, Piper has an acute case of chronic giggles, and Paige can barely stay awake. Maybe our powers aren't the only thing that's being affected by . . . whatever's going on."

"But I haven't run into anything weird either," Paige said. "No demons or warlocks or anything else that reeks of diabolical intent."

"That you know of." Piper fought back the laughter rumbling in her throat. The situation wasn't funny, and yet . . . it was.

"Good point." Phoebe sighed. "Our evil adversaries don't always advertise their presence or their agenda."

"Maybe it's something that doesn't have an agenda," Leo said. "There's been so much active magic practiced in this house over the years, maybe the same residual factors that lured the gremlin attracted some other magical contaminant."

"What?" Piper started. "Like hocus-pocus pollen?"

"An abracadabra allergy?" Paige grinned.

"It's possible," Leo said. "We've got a gremlin."

"Time to hit the book." Phoebe jumped up and dashed behind the pedestal that held *The Book of Shadows*. She flipped though the pages, then paused. "What am I looking for?"

"Something to isolate any new magical elements in the house." Piper scrambled to her feet and nudged Phoebe aside. "It'll be faster if I look."

"Wake me when you find something." Paige set the pin bowl aside and curled up on the carpet.

Leo began moving boxes, clearing a path to the small radiator that kept the chill off the attic during the winter.

Phoebe turned to stare out the front window.

Piper didn't try to keep the inane smile off her face as she searched through the book. A little levity was a welcome change from the undercurrent of doom and gloom that usually defined their lives. They had dealt with so many lethal, dark forces since becoming the Charmed Ones; an infestation of pixie dust or magical microbes was nothing but an amusing irritation.

"This might work." Piper looked up from a back page titled "Miscellaneous Entities, Substances, Incantations, and Cures." Like so many topics contained in the Halliwells' ever-changing *Book of Shadows*, the miscellany reference pages appeared to be recent additions.

Paige shifted position but didn't wake up.

"Pardon me?" Phoebe glanced back, her dark brown eyes wide and questioning.

Leo braced his foot against the pipe attached to the bottom of the radiator and tightened the wrench around a stuck valve on top of the connector. Engrossed in the plumbing problem, he didn't hear her.

"Never mind." Exhaling, Piper smoothed the page. "I can do this with the Power of One."

Taking a deep breath, Piper began to recite a simple spell to unmask minor magical agents.

> *Unknown magics on mystic tides that*
> *breached the darkened gate;*
> *lost bits and beings, seek and hide,*
> *now reveal and locate.*

Phoebe turned expectantly.

Piper tensed, waiting.

"Got it!" Leo raised a triumphant fist. As he leaned over to shut the loosened valve, a high-pitched shriek erupted from inside the radiator.

"I think you found something," Phoebe said.

Right, Piper thought as she darted across the

attic. She didn't have time to refresh Phoebe's memory. The gremlin wasn't reacting to the spell, but to the closing valve that would trap it inside the radiator. "Hurry, Leo! Before it gets away!"

"I'm trying!" The muscles in Leo's arms bulged as he turned the resisting knob.

That valve probably hasn't been closed in decades, Piper thought. Since it was only a matter of seconds before the critter realized an escape route was still open, she tried to freeze it inside the radiator. Her ineffectual magic only heightened its rage.

"What's going on?" Phoebe covered her ears to muffle the gremlin's piercing screams.

"Gremlin!" Piper's shouted reply reverberated off the rafters. The creature's shrill cry faded as it fled downward through the pipes.

"It's gone." Muttering under his breath, Leo finished closing the valve.

"Thank goodness." Rubbing her temples, Phoebe stumbled back to the rocker. She almost tripped over Paige. "How could she sleep through that?"

"I wish I knew." Blowing a wisp of hair off her forehead, Piper sighed. "Before I get laughing so hard I can't talk, here's what I think we should do."

"Rise and shine, Paige." Phoebe shook the sleeping witch awake. "One of us has to know what she's talking about."

"The I.D. spell didn't work?" Leo asked.

"That's one possibility." Piper was almost certain the spell had worked fine, but she couldn't be one hundred percent positive. "Or there aren't any magical contaminants in the house to find, which is my best guess."

"Then we still don't know what's interfering with our powers." Paige stretched.

"You got it." Piper clamped her lips closed to smother another laugh. When it subsided, she continued. "So, since no innocents need us to save them right now, we should stop using our powers until we figure out the problem."

"Okay," Phoebe said. "This is probably the first time in my life I won't mind being grounded."

"Good one." Piper chuckled.

"Sounds reasonable," Paige said, "but for all we know, stress and fatigue *are* responsible."

"That's not likely." Leo handed Piper the wrench. "Maybe I'd better check with the Elders."

"I second that idea," Paige said. "They wouldn't appreciate being kept out of the loop anyway."

"Heaven forbid." Piper kissed Leo on the cheek and waved as he dissolved into swirls of blue light.

"What about my visions?" Phoebe asked anxiously. "I can't just *decide* to turn off the psychic antenna."

"No, but since you won't remember what you

see long enough to tell us about it, that's almost the same as not having a vision," Piper said.

Paige frowned. "Which means we won't know if Phoebe contacts an innocent who's being threatened by a demon."

"Then the powers that be will find another way to let us know," Piper said. "They always do."

"Let's hope they don't have to," Phoebe said. "Without our powers, we won't be much help to anyone."

Piper nodded while she tried not to laugh. As Paige had pointed out, there wasn't anything funny about the unexplained loss of potency in their powers. If some denizen of the dark threatened them or an innocent, it might be fatal.

Chapter

4

"Paige!" Lila whispered loudly from the copy room doorway.

"Huh?" Paige looked up from the stack of forms lying on the copy machine. Hawthorn Hill Home had promised to speed up processing Stanley Addison's application if she sent all the additional information they needed immediately. Since the home's fax machine wasn't working, she was making copies to messenger over.

"Is something wrong with the copier?" Lila asked. "You've been in here for half an hour."

"No, everything's fine." *Sort of*, Paige thought as she lifted the copier lid, removed one of Stanley's Social Security forms, and slipped another original onto the plate. She hadn't fallen asleep on her feet. She had just been staring into space in a daze, which was almost as bad. "Can you wait five more minutes to use the machine? I'm almost done."

"I don't need any copies," Lila said. "You've got a visitor."

"Sister? Client?" Paige craned her neck, but she couldn't see into her cubicle.

"Cute guy with a cane," Lila said.

"Kevin Graves?" Paige blinked. *What is he doing here?* "Tell him I'll be right there, okay?"

Although she was dying of curiosity, Paige finished copying Stanley's info and stuffed the pages into an envelope she had already addressed. She left it with the receptionist to be picked up by the messenger, then walked back to her desk and tried not to appear *too* anxious.

Kevin sat in the client chair, nervously tapping his rubber-tipped cane on the floor. He flashed her a megawatt smile when she entered. "Hi, Paige."

"This is a surprise." *Did I totally misread Kevin's lack of interest the past two nights?* Paige wondered as she dropped into her chair. It was hard to believe someone with his good looks and muscular physique was shy, but life was full of oddities.

"This isn't a problem, is it?" Kevin's smile shifted into a look of worried uncertainty. "Coming to see you at your job, I mean."

"No, not at all," Paige said, fudging the truth. If Mr. Cowan asked, she could honestly say she and Kevin both volunteered at the Fifth Street Shelter, which was social services related. "What can I do for you?"

"Well, I, uh—" Kevin reached into his front pocket and pulled out a pair of black, wrap-around sunglasses. "Are these yours? I found them in my car."

"Not mine," Paige said. She didn't have to examine the expensive, designer lenses to know they weren't hers.

"Oh." Kevin hesitated, shrugging. "I thought maybe they fell out of your purse when I drove you home the other night."

"Sorry, no." Paige had no idea what Kevin was up to. He had been friendly at the shelter last night, but the mutual tension she had felt Monday night hadn't been there.

Kevin heaved a long sigh, then looked at her from under thick, dark eyelashes. "Okay, I didn't find them."

Paige arched an eyebrow, but didn't interrupt.

"They're mine." Kevin slipped the glasses into his shirt pocket. "I just needed an excuse to see you again. Pretty dumb, huh?"

"Definitely dumb," Paige agreed. "You didn't need an excuse to see me."

"But now I've blown it, right?" Using his cane for support, Kevin stood up and perched on the corner of the desk.

"I don't like being lied to, but—"

"So let me make it up to you." Kevin cocked his head and leaned toward her, gently touching her leg with the end of his cane. "I'd give anything if I could take you dancing, but since that's not possible . . ."

Paige swayed slightly.

". . . how about dinner Saturday night instead?" Kevin jerked his cane back, as though he had just noticed he was caressing her calf with the rubber tip. Embarrassed, he slid off the desk. "At least think about it? I'll, uh . . . see you later, at the shelter."

"Uh, sure." Paige nodded. "Okay." When her head cleared a moment later, he was gone.

Sighing, Paige dropped her head onto her folded arms. She probably should have just accepted Kevin's invitation. Being a witch had put a serious damper on the dating part of her life, and there was no telling how long it would be before someone else asked her out.

Yawning, she forced one eye open to look at her watch. It was only 3:10 in the afternoon, but she was exhausted. She felt as though she had been up all night, when she had actually slept a solid nine hours. In fact, she had over-slept again and had barely made it to work on time.

Paige snapped her head up when she started to doze off. She'd be in big trouble if Mr. Cowan caught her sleeping on the job. As she set Stanley's file aside, her gaze fell on her watch.

With almost two hours left until five o'clock and another four hours of shelter duty to go before she could go home to bed, Paige needed a

major infusion of wake-up juice. She glanced at
the small cactus she had transferred into
Grams's pin bowl on her lunch hour, then
grabbed a mug and headed for the coffee station.

Piper sat at the bar making out next week's bev-
erage order as she did every Wednesday. Today,
however, she was not alone. With a Vengeance
had arrived at two o'clock sharp to set up for
their San Francisco debut the following night. If
the rehearsal session was any indication, they
would be a smash hit. Every song the group had
practiced was on the current charts.

When she finished, Piper set the order aside
to call in later. Turning sideways, she propped
her feet on another stool and gave the band her
full attention. Since Dixie was still using the high
school baby-sitter with the strict curfew, the bar
needed to be swept out, wiped down, and
stocked, but that could wait another ten minutes.

Piper hummed along to a classic rock tune
that bemoaned the fleeting euphoria of new
love. Ironically, a relaxed attitude and good
mood seemed to be side effects of chronic laughing syndrome.

Daniel sang with his eyes closed and his head
thrown back, pouring emotion into the plaintive
words. ". . . what we're feeling now will pass,
fading like the day gives way to night; like whis-
pers on the wind, no love can last . . ."

Piper was struck by the pessimism of the song's sentiment. Whoever had written it obviously didn't understand that love faced constant trials. Only true love survived them.

As his husky voice sustained the final note, Daniel looked up from the keyboard, caught Piper's eye, and winked. As the last chord faded, he pointed at her, and then at himself with a quizzical, come-on expression.

Flattered, Piper raised her left hand. She pointed to her wedding ring and laughed when Daniel adopted an exaggerated look of disappointment. Then he shrugged and ran his fingers over the keys.

Karen glanced at Daniel and rolled her eyes as she jumped off the stage. Her grin widened as she approached the bar. "Daniel doesn't believe in being subtle."

"I noticed." Piper giggled, sharing the boys-can-be-such-a-pain moment with the other woman. Still, the harmless flirtation reminded her of Leo and how much she missed him. Hours had passed for her since he left last night, but only minutes had elapsed for him "up there."

Karen flipped open the flute case she had left on the bar. "I promise I won't forget to take this onstage with me this weekend. I'm a little overprotective because it's so old."

"I thought it looked like an antique." Piper noticed that part of the pattern etched into the wood was red. She didn't remember it being red on Monday. "It's beautiful."

"Thanks." As Karen leaned over the bar to grab a cocktail napkin, the flute touched the side of Piper's face.

Piper's skin tingled as another wave of light-headedness washed over her.

"One more song and we'll call it quits for today. You've probably got a lot to do before opening." Using the napkin to wipe her brow, Karen headed back to the stage.

"Yeah, sure." Piper closed her eyes and took a deep breath. The dizziness subsided when the band launched into their last number a moment later.

As Lancer struck a minor chord, Brodie hit the cymbals. The sustained sound of brass and bass faded as the clear, mournful tones of the flute filled the empty room.

Piper sighed, wishing Leo would get back soon so she'd know *exactly* what she should worry about. There was nothing funny or normal about being amused by everything. Although it seemed likely the unknown force that had weakened her power was to blame, it was possible the crushing burdens of being a Charmed One had finally pushed her over the edge into a merry disconnect.

So I'm either insane or cursed, Piper thought, her spirits plunging. What kind of choice was that? *None*, she realized as she slipped off the stool and trudged behind the bar to set up for the early evening shift.

Karen stopped playing the flute to blend her low, contralto voice with Daniel's tenor. When they finished, the boys high-fived one another and began packing their instruments.

Piper made a mental note to make sure Karen spaced the slow ballads and sad songs farther apart when the band debuted tomorrow night. Downer moods were bad for business.

"Let's stop by that Spoons No Soup place for an early dinner," Brodie suggested. "The bartender at Jay's Joint was raving about the food last night."

Piper almost interrupted to explain that the stingy portions at the popular yuppie restaurant were overpriced and overhyped. She could whip up a better menu in her sleep, but she didn't say a word. She felt as though the worries of the whole world had crash-landed on her shoulders and she was too weary to talk.

"It's not even four o'clock yet," Daniel said. "If I eat now, I'll be hungry again by ten."

Lancer shrugged and picked up his bass. "I can do dinner twice."

"A salad sounds good to me." Karen waved the guys out the door and stepped over to the bar. "We'll see you tomorrow night, then, Piper. About eight thirty. I like to mingle for a few minutes to get a feel for the crowd before we start."

"Sure." Piper forced a smile as Karen placed her flute back in the case and snapped it closed. "Banjo's has great salads. Steaks and burgers, too, and it won't cost you a small fortune. Three blocks that way." She pointed and stiffened self-consciously under the singer's probing stare.

"Thanks," Karen said finally. A subtle frown erased her bland expression for a brief moment. Then, apparently sensing that Piper didn't want to prolong the small talk, she nodded and left.

The instant the door closed, leaving her alone, Piper began to sob. Grabbing a bunch of cocktail napkins, she sank to the floor and gave in to the tears.

Phoebe stared at the computer screen, clueless. For a fleeting instant, she actually wished that all the forces of the underworld had suddenly united against her and her sisters. Dealing with a magical something that was trying to make her crazy would be marginally better than being driven daft by her own faulty memory.

Except that the two are probably connected, she thought.

Phoebe scowled. Piper had called her cell phone just before class to say that Leo had come home from the great beyond above. She had sounded upset, which wasn't hard to understand. The Elders were mystified by her and her sisters' emotional, physical, and magical afflictions and unaware of any new imminent threat.

They were checking the archives for similar incidents or references, but without more specific information, the effort might be futile. Leo had orbed out again to see if he could pick up anything on the demonic street.

Phoebe shared the Elders' apprehension. Anything that affected the Charmed Ones' powers was a matter of grave concern. Still, she couldn't help but wonder if emotional stress was the cause of her problem. At the university, she had read dozens of case studies about people who had developed severe physical ailments as a result of intense pressure at home or work. Couldn't pressure affect her ability to function as a witch?

Her romantic history definitely fit the pattern.

Loving Cole had dealt her one serious emotional blow after another: from the normal uncertainties in the beginning—was the tall, dark, handsome D.A. as interested in her as she was in him?—to finding out he had a demon half called Belthazor who was trying to kill her and her sisters, then lying to her sisters about vanquishing him when she hadn't, and finally having to deal with his emotional traumas because he was human and powerless.

Lots of people have gone mad with less reason, Phoebe thought matter-of-factly. Of course, her sisters were also experiencing bizarre effects, and they weren't in love with Cole.

The realization that she was in danger of losing her powers without knowing why hit Phoebe hard. Suddenly she could really empathize with Cole's difficulty adjusting to being human. Although he needed his fishing getaway to work things out, she wished he would come home. She needed the moral support.

"Setting up tables involves more initial steps and headaches," Mr. Deekle said dryly, "but using them will save you time, and maybe even customers, in the end. Can anyone tell us why?"

Phoebe read over the numbered instructions for sizing and implanting tables in a Web page, but they might as well have been written in ancient Sanskrit. By the time she read step number eight, she had forgotten step number one. Creativity might be the key to a successful career in Web design, but having cool ideas was fast becoming a moot point. If she couldn't remember basic technical information, she wasn't even going to get through the course.

"Ms. Halliwell?" The professor's beady eyes widened with expectation when she looked up.

"Uh—what was the question?" Phoebe asked lamely.

"Didn't read the assigned pages, did we?" Deekle's thin lips compressed into an accusing smile.

"Actually, I did," Phoebe stammered, "but I don't—"

The professor dismissed her excuse without letting her finish. He turned and pointed toward a young man with glasses in the next row. "Mr. Harrison?"

Kate was sitting behind Phoebe. She leaned forward and whispered, "Don't let that jerk get you down, Phoebe."

"What jerk?" Phoebe glanced at Professor Deekle, who was listening intently to a young man with glasses in the next row. "Him?"

"Who else?" Kate said softly. "A good instructor wouldn't make his students so nervous, they can't answer his questions."

Phoebe just nodded. "Maybe my luck will hold and he won't call on me."

"You can hope," Kate said.

The touch of cold metal against her neck caught Phoebe by surprise. "What was that?"

"What?" Kate asked, obviously perplexed.

"Huh?" Phoebe glanced back, feeling almost as confused as Kate looked. "Did you say something?"

"Nope." Kate smiled. "Not a word."

Chapter
5

Leo materialized in the kitchen of the Halliwell's Victorian house with nothing to report. The evil grapevine was as uninformed as the Elders, with no buzz of a new demonic plot to defeat the Charmed Ones or to take over the world. *Not this week anyway*, Leo thought as he glanced around. Apparently the past eighteen hours in the Manor had not been nearly as uneventful as his snooping expedition.

Piper's culinary domain was a disaster.

Various magical and menu ingredients were spilled and scattered across the table and counters. Cabinet doors stood open, dishes were broken, and puddles of water had formed under leaks in the ceiling. A pot of something foul bubbled on the stove, and an unidentifiable burned casserole had been dumped on the floor.

The mess was his first clue that something

was terribly wrong. The second was realizing that the usual peace and quiet had been replaced by blaring TV noise.

A movement in the sink caught Leo's eye. The smaller basin was full of fruits and vegetables that had been mashed into pulp and topped off with a package of saltine crackers. He froze when the gremlin popped out of the drain in the other sink and dove into the vegetable slush.

Leo slowly slipped a dish towel free of a cabinet handle. He hardly dared breathe for fear of alerting the creature, which was making contented cooing sounds as it dug through the pile of garbage. Wrapping the towel around his hand like a mitt, Leo braced to pounce. He just had to grab the slippery gremlin and hold on long enough to orb. Then he could set it free back in the underworld, where it belonged.

Just before Leo made his move, the gremlin burrowed into its disgusting lunch and disappeared. Having missed his chance to capture the intruder, Leo tossed the towel on the counter. Hearing a slurping noise, he looked into the sink as he turned to leave. A curl of grapefruit rind vanished into the mess.

"Piper!" Leo followed the boisterous sound of a game show announcer's voice listing potential prizes. He found Piper sitting on the living room sofa, absently stirring gray goo in a large wooden bowl, and staring at the TV. Tears rolled down her face.

"Piper?" Leo kneeled in front of her. Last night she had tried to hide her distress when he had told her that no big-time evil magic was going down anywhere that the Elders were aware of. He hadn't realized then that she had done a complete emotional one-eighty from happy to depressed. "What's wrong?"

Piper sniffled and wiped her damp cheek with the back of her hand. "Millie lost."

"Millie?" Leo frowned, uncomprehending, until Piper waved her spoon at the TV. He jerked back to avoid splatters of gray goop that shook loose. "On the show?"

Piper nodded, more tears pouring from her dark eyes. "Millie wanted the fishing boat for her grandson, so she just kept playing instead of settling for the big-screen TV and entertainment center. But then she missed the big question, so now she doesn't get anything except a year's supply of some stupid laundry detergent that's not nearly as good as the sponsor says it is."

"A real tragedy." Leo wasn't sure what to say. He tried changing the subject, hoping the diversion would have a calming effect. "What are you making?"

"A vitamin potion for Gilbert." Piper inhaled, shuddering as she held back another teary outburst.

"Gilbert?" Leo blinked. "That wouldn't happen to be the gremlin, would it?"

Piper nodded again.

"And you're feeding it?" Leo asked aghast.

"Don't you dare yell at me, Leo Wyatt!" Piper's eyes blazed, but her mouth quivered. "I had to do *something* to keep him busy until you figure out how to catch him. Have you seen the laundry room?"

Leo shook his head. "Is it worse than the kitchen?"

Piper leaned closer, lowering her voice. "He pulverized that big metal hose that goes to the dryer vent."

"What was a plumbing gremlin doing in the dryer?" Leo asked.

"Throwing a temper tantrum, obviously," Piper snapped.

"Obviously." It was also obvious to Leo that Piper's depressed state of mind had worsened since last night. They had much bigger problems than an annoyed gremlin. "Is Phoebe here?"

Piper pointed the spoon up. "Attic. Since we don't really think plain old-fashioned nervous breakdowns are why I'm a basket case and her mind has turned into a sieve, she's checking *The Book of Shadows* for a magical explanation."

"Don't move," Leo gently ordered. "I'll be right back."

Piper picked up the remote and changed channels as he dissolved into light for a quick trip upstairs.

● ● ●

"Hey, Leo. What's up?" Phoebe sat cross-legged on the attic floor sorting the contents of an old trunk.

"Piper said you were checking the book." Leo glanced toward the pedestal. *The Book of Shadows* was closed.

"Checking for what?" Phoebe folded an embroidered dresser scarf and placed it on a pile of decorative linens.

"Why you can't remember what you're doing from one minute to the next." Leo paused as the complications inherent in Phoebe's condition sank in. "So checking the book is a pointless exercise for you, isn't it?"

"That makes perfect sense." Phoebe pulled a pink, monogrammed baby sweater out of the trunk. "Should I be worried?"

"Why bother when you won't recall what you're worried about?" Leo smiled, but he was worried enough for both of them. "I need your help right now though."

"Okay." Phoebe rose and dusted off her jeans. The loosely crocheted sweater she wore over a T-shirt captured her gaze. She held up her arm to study the long, bell-shaped sleeves. "Where did this come from? It's gorgeous."

"From that trunk probably." Leo grabbed her hand and started for the door. "Come on. I need your help."

"What's the problem?" Phoebe asked.

"I'll explain after we get downstairs so I only

have to go over it once." Leo motioned Phoebe through the door. By the time they reached the living room, she had no recollection of the conversation they had just had in the attic.

"What are you watching?" Phoebe asked Piper.

"Some soap opera called *Where All Roads End*." Piper dabbed her moist eyes with the hem of her shirt. "How can people watch this stuff every day? Nothing ever goes right for anybody."

"Sounds vaguely familiar," Phoebe muttered.

Leo took the bowl of gremlin vitamins away from Piper. She had stirred it so long, the mixture had turned into lumpy gray soup. "Where's your laptop, Phoebe?"

"I don't know." Phoebe glanced around. "I don't see it anywhere."

Piper stood up and poked Leo in the chest. "You give Gilbert his Piper pick-me-up. I'll find the laptop."

"Piper—" Leo paused to curb his exasperation. Usually he had the proverbial patience of a saint, but then again, usually the Charmed Ones weren't acting like insipid airheads. "Have either of you tried using your powers today?"

"Don't know," Phoebe said.

Piper shook her head. "We decided not to, remember?"

"We did?" Phoebe looked confused. "When?"

"When doesn't matter, Phoebe," Leo said. "Try levitating now."

"Sure." Phoebe breathed in deeply. When her feet were still on the floor a moment later, she gritted her teeth and squinted her eyes closed. The increased concentration helped her rise a few inches off the floor. She hovered for several seconds before gravity overpowered her magic and pulled her back down.

"That cannot possibly be good." Piper bit her lip.

"I'm home." Paige walked in, dropped her bag on the floor, and flopped down on the sofa Piper had just vacated.

"Aren't you early?" Piper looked at her watch and started to sob. "It's only four o'clock, Paige. Mr. Cowan didn't fire you, did he? What's that going to do to our budget?"

"Nothing." Paige yawned. "He sent me home sick."

"Do you have a fever?" Phoebe placed her hand on Paige's forehead.

Paige brushed it away. "No, I'm having such a hard time staying awake, Mr. Cowan is sure I've got the flu. He wanted me out of the office before I infected everyone else."

"That's actually the first stroke of good luck we've had today," Leo said. At least when Paige was awake, she had control of her thoughts and impulses.

"Bad day all around?" Paige propped an eye open with her fingers.

"Probably." Sighing, Phoebe perched on the

arm of the couch. "I can barely get my feet off the ground."

"Bummer." Paige dropped her head on a throw pillow, and her eyelids fluttered closed. "But I thought we weren't going to use our powers until we know why they aren't working right."

"Really?" Phoebe covered her mouth. "Oops."

"I've got a theory about the power loss," Leo said. He didn't want to say anything more until he had supporting evidence. "Try freezing something, Piper."

"Okay." Sniffling, Piper snapped her hands toward the TV. The images on the screen didn't pause but began to move in slow motion. "Uh-oh."

"Is freezing supposed to work like that?" Phoebe asked.

Piper frowned. "No, but maybe my explode mode is okay."

Before Leo could question the wisdom of a blowup test using faulty powers, Piper zapped a potted plant in the window. It wasn't obliterated. The leaves just wilted and the flower petals fell off.

"That's way worse than yesterday, isn't it?" Paige turned on to her side facing the room.

"Hard to say." Piper shrugged. "I didn't try to blow up anything yesterday."

"Your turn, Paige," Leo said.

A brittle tension gripped the room as Paige sat up and flexed her fingers. She hesitated and then went for it with a bold thrust of her hand. "Remote!"

Leo frowned when nothing happened immediately. A moment later, the remote control slowly dissolved into orb particles, which drifted into Paige's hand and slowly re-formed.

"Well, that didn't go exactly as I expected," Paige said.

"Can I see that?" Leo took the remote from Paige's hand. At first glance the device seemed fine. On closer inspection, he noticed that the lettering formed nonsense words and the buttons were out of line.

"Oh, boy." Paige winced when Leo pointed out the flaws in the remote. "That's definitely worse than yesterday."

"Which is what I wanted to find out." Leo kept his tone matter-of-fact when the three sisters looked to him for clarification. "Something happened to start the power drain in the first place, and whatever it was, it happened to each of you again since yesterday."

Although Phoebe looked more perplexed than Piper and Paige, they were all baffled.

"But nothing happened," Paige insisted.

"Yes, it did," Leo said firmly. "Nothing else can account for the diminished powers and the excessive physical and emotional side effects you're all experiencing."

"I'm at a loss." Phoebe rubbed her temples.

"Me too," Piper sobbed.

Paige wasn't convinced either. "But that implies that we've all been exposed to the same thing, Leo. That's a little hard to believe, since the only time we've been together is here."

"Gilbert!" Piper gasped.

"Who's Gilbert?" Paige asked.

"Piper named the gremlin," Leo explained, "but gremlins don't have powers that can directly affect anyone, good or evil. They just have magical properties that make it possible for them to disrupt inanimate things, like World War Two airplanes and plumbing."

"You *named* the gremlin?" Paige glared at Piper.

"Forget Gilbert for now," Leo said. "He's not responsible for your problems. Something is though, and we've got to figure out what before you don't have any powers left."

"Any ideas?" Paige asked hopefully.

"Not many." Leo shook his head. "Only that you've all encountered something in the past few days that you've never run into before. And whatever it was, you came into contact with it twice."

Paige tried to shake off the gremlin that was gnawing on her leg, but the ugly little beast just sank his fangs in deeper.

"Come on, Paige."

"Huh? What—" Paige awoke from the dream with a start. Phoebe was shaking her knee.

"It's almost seven," Phoebe said. "Time to get up."

"Why?" Moaning, Paige drew her knees to her chest and threw an arm over her head. She was still on the couch, where she had been left to slumber undisturbed since the family meeting that afternoon.

"Uh—" Phoebe cleared her throat. "Wait a sec while I check."

Curious, Paige rolled over to look at her sister through half-opened eyes. She didn't recognize the delicately crocheted sweater Phoebe was wearing. The garment had a 1960s hippie look that went perfectly with her sister's T-shirt and jeans. "Nice sweater. Did you find it at a thrift shop?"

"Let's see." Phoebe sat on the coffee table with her laptop on her lap. She silently mouthed the words she was reading, then said, "Attic. What was the other question?"

"Why do I have to wake up?" Paige repeated.

"Oh, right." Phoebe glanced back at the screen and smiled. "Because Piper's making dinner and Leo wants you to check *The Book of Shadows*. I'm not much help in the research department right now."

"Whose idea was it to use the computer as a substitute memory?" Paige pushed herself upright and swung her feet to the floor. Her eyelids felt as though someone had glued lead weights to her lashes.

"Not sure." Phoebe shrugged. "Probably Leo's. Works really well, too." She glanced back at the screen. "It looks like we made a whole list of stuff I need to remember."

"I'm impressed," Paige said. "Does your list include what Leo wants me to look for in the book?"

"No, but"—Phoebe ran her finger down the list—"*The Book of Shadows* is in the kitchen, which Leo and Piper just finished cleaning."

"And they let me sleep?" Paige stretched to work out the kinks in her muscles, then smoothed her wrinkled skirt. "Must be my lucky day."

"Don't think so," Phoebe said as she followed Paige into the hall. "According to my list, Piper is devastated because you ruined the remote control."

"Really?" Paige cast an annoyed look back at Phoebe. "How does she feel about almost killing a plant?"

Paige headed straight for the refrigerator and pulled out a bottled juice. Piper and Leo must have cleaned to keep their minds off the current problem, which had no known cause or solution. The kitchen looked just as it had that morning, in perfect order except for a huge pile of garbage in one half of the double sink. "Did Gilbert break the garbage disposal?"

"I'm not going to turn it on to find out." Piper poured some gray goop on top of the garbage, then put the wooden bowl in the empty sink and filled it with water. Her eyes were red from crying. "We've got enough problems without adding ground gremlin to the list."

"We have a gremlin? Shouldn't that be on *my* list?" Phoebe settled in at the table and muttered as she typed. "'Do not turn on garbage disposal. Gremlin in it and would be really messy.'"

"I hope you can stay awake awhile after your nap, Paige." Leo finished stacking coffee cups in a cabinet and closed the dishwasher.

"I'll try." Yawning, Paige took a chair opposite Phoebe and flipped open *The Book of Shadows*. "Can you give me a hint what to look for?"

"Sorry." Leo shook his head. "If there's something there, I'm hoping you'll know it when you see it."

Paige nodded and began turning pages. The Halliwell family's book of magical lore was in constant flux, always with purpose, usually by the hand of an ancestor. Information pertinent to new dangers had a tendency to show up when they needed it. She just hoped the book didn't let them down now.

"There's a really weird reference on my laptop about a gremlin in the garbage disposal." Phoebe looked over her shoulder at Leo and Piper. "Is there anything else about gremlins I should know?"

"Yes." Piper picked up the cordless phone. "If the sink runs low on gremlin garbage chow, refill it. Does anyone care what I order from Sun Li's Chinese Takeout?"

"Sweet-and-sour anything," Phoebe said.

Paige cocked a quizzical eyebrow. Apparently, Phoebe's long-term memory was intact and unaffected. Since the computer compensated for the short-term deficiency, she was remarkably functional under the circumstances.

"Egg rolls and crab Rangoon." Leo pulled up a chair. "Better make that a double order. I'm starved."

"The shelter!" Paige suddenly stood up. "I'm supposed to be working at the shelter tonight."

"I called Doug and told him you weren't feeling well," Leo said. "Seemed like the logical thing to do."

"Since I can't serve food and sleep at the same time, it was. Thanks." Paige sat back down. Resting her chin in her hand, she went back to turning pages. "I hope Jennifer and Kevin showed, so Doug's not shorthanded."

"Couldn't be helped. Phoebe's skipping her class, and I bailed on P3 tonight, too. Nobody's going anywhere until"—Piper blinked back more tears—"we have some answers. Excuse me." She pulled Sun Li's paper menu out of a drawer and disappeared into the hall with the cordless phone.

Paige felt herself drifting off and shook her head. "This is getting old fast. . . ." She stopped to stare at a page she didn't remember seeing before.

"Find something?" Leo leaned over to look.

"Maybe. This rhymes, but it doesn't seem to be a spell." Paige frowned as she scanned the four-line entry.

"You're sure it's not an incantation?" Leo asked.

Nodding, Paige read the passage aloud. "'And should the chosen three of evil be awakened/ the champions of virtue must defend/the light of ages past or be forsaken/ as the warriors of darkness were before them.'"

"Any clue what it means?" Phoebe typed the verse into her laptop before she forgot it.

"Not really, but it's more to go on than we had before." Rising, Leo glanced toward the hall. "Tell Piper I've gone to consult the Elders again."

"Right." Phoebe nodded as her fingers pounded the keys. "'Tell Piper Leo gone to Elders.' Got it."

After Leo orbed out, Paige laid her head on the book and closed her eyes. "Don't forget to hit 'save.'"

"I'll make a note."

Paige was asleep before Phoebe finished typing.

Chapter

6

karen dropped her leather jacket on a chair as Kevin closed the apartment door behind her. "Where's Kate?"

"Right here!" The younger woman stuck her head out of a small kitchen. She flashed a brilliant smile and waved a large knife.

"Honing up on your combat skills, Ce'kahn?" Karen asked with pointed sarcasm.

"*Kate* brought pizza." Kevin reinforced *his* point with a cold stare, an unspoken reminder that their clan names must remain secret until after they vanquished the Sol'agath.

"I think better on a full stomach," Kate said.

"What's the emergency?" Karen asked abruptly.

Kevin met the musician's hard gaze. Once known as Sh'tara and soon to be known as Sh'tara again, Karen wouldn't argue with him.

The ancient master sorcerer who had arranged their escape from a miserable fate had designated him, Tov'reh, as their leader. Neither of his companion warriors would defy Shen'arch's will or wisdom.

When Karen had finally met him and Kate at the appointed place two years ago, he had insisted that they continue the pretense of their human lives. Raised in normal families and college educated, they had developed careers and social contacts as adults. Consequently they had left no suspicious gaps in their backgrounds that might alert the Sol'agath's ancestors to their true nature and purpose. They had also taken great care to make sure their old Dor'chacht names could not be used by the higher powers to link them to the past.

"Even the old warriors of darkness had to eat," Kevin joked to ease the sting of his rebuke.

"Yeah, but we didn't have the convenience of takeout back then." Kate hurried in carrying a cardboard container with a steaming pizza.

"I don't want to be late to P3." Karen eyed the American combination of bread, cheese, meat, and tomato sauce with disgust. "Besides, I miss the taste of wild boar cooked over an open flame."

"Yuck." Kate knelt by the coffee table and gingerly lifted a triangle of pizza onto a paper plate. "I'll take hamburgers, shrimp scampi, and caesar salad with broiled chicken over half-cooked, stringy pig meat any day."

"Enough talk about food. We've got a problem and not much time to fix it." Kevin pushed a stack of newspapers off a worn sofa that dominated the center of the room, and motioned for Karen to sit.

"Does it have anything to do with why Kate's not at her computer class and you're not at the shelter, Kevin?" Karen perched on the edge of the couch and placed her flute case in her lap.

Kevin watched as Karen's gaze shifted from the paper plates and napkins on the coffee table to the TV and satellite receiver resting on a metal stand. A state-of-the-art computer sat on the desk against the opposite wall. He knew that she had always felt estranged in the late twentieth century, while he had easily adapted to the faster pace, technological innovations, and customs of the modern world.

Kate's interest in men, food, and sporting fun was just as appropriate in the present as it had been three thousand years ago.

"Paige didn't show up at the shelter," Kevin said.

"And Phoebe was a no-show at the college." Kate took a bite of pizza.

Karen tensed. "Do you think the Sol'agath witches have figured out what's going on?"

"How could they?" Kate wiped a string of cheese off her chin. "Shen'arch said the higher powers wouldn't be able to detect us as long as we're human, and we'll be human until tomor-row night—after we're in the Valley of Ages and it's too late to stop us."

Karen closed her eyes and tilted her face upward, a gesture of honor for the long-dead master Dor'chacht sorcerer.

And our powers are dormant in the artifacts, Kevin thought. The powerful elders above and the demonic elements below couldn't detect inert magic, either, especially when it hadn't been used in three millennia. Time and Shen'arch's unsurpassed craft had served their cause well.

"Doug said Paige's brother-in-law called her in sick," Kevin explained. "Since her fatigue level increases each time the cane drains her power, I'm inclined to believe that."

"Phoebe probably forgot she *had* a class." Kate laughed. "Last night she didn't remember five seconds later that Mr. Deekle had called on her to answer a question, and that was *before* I touched her a second time."

"I wouldn't be surprised to find out that Piper's gotten suspicious." Frowning, Karen absently rubbed the flute case. "How could she not notice that she's gone from being always amused to totally depressed for no reason, or that her power has been depleted?"

"But she might not connect that with touch-ing the flute," Kate said.

Maybe, maybe not, Kevin thought. The tunes Karen played on her flute had influenced Piper because she was a witch. A temporary magical bond had been formed when the instrument had siphoned off a measured portion of her power. Humans were immune. The side effects inflicted by his cane and Kate's bracelet on Paige and Phoebe were a lot easier to explain away. However, the witches' fatigue, forgetfulness, and manic moods may have kept the Charmed Ones from uncovering the Dor'chacht plot just as Shen'arch had intended.

But even if Piper has figured it out, Kevin thought, *it's too late to help her.*

"I'll know if we've blown our cover when I see Piper at P3," Karen said. "Either way, I'll make sure she touches the flute again." Her eyes narrowed as she looked up. "But that doesn't solve your problem. You've both got to tap Phoebe and Paige a third time before the battle begins."

"I'm going to drop by Phoebe's house to lend her the notes from tonight's class." Kate pulled a paper napkin off her sticky fingers. "We've hung out and gotten friendly, so I don't think she'll question it."

Karen looked at Kate askance. "You didn't go to class tonight."

Kate rolled her eyes. "No, but Stuart Randall did, and he's taking notes for me. We're going out later, and he said we could stop by the Halliwell house on our way to the movie."

"You've got a date?" Karen asked, aghast. "Tonight?"

"What?" Kate's perky face puckered into a playful pout. "I can't have a boyfriend after we become the most powerful magical force in the world?"

Kevin shifted uneasily, dismayed by Kate's cavalier attitude. Unwavering focus and conviction were essential in the upcoming duel with Paige and her sisters, the latest, most powerful witches in the Sol'agath line. The Dor'chacht had challenged the Halliwells' ancestors thirty centuries before, hoping to exterminate the Sol'agath and their benevolent magic, but they had vastly underestimated the power of good. That battle had been lost, but now the Dor'chacht's long awaited chance for vengeance was imminent.

Kevin breathed deeply to cement his resolve. Transported across time by Shen'arch's last-minute spell, he had emerged twenty-six years ago with the humiliation of defeat buried and burning within. If they failed this time, there would be no more chances to regain the Dor'chacht clan's lost magic and position of power. Their mental, spiritual, and emotional matrixes would die, leaving mindless, comatose bodies behind to confound anyone who had known them.

But they would not lose, Kevin vowed. Their enraged desire for vengeance combined with experience gave them an edge they hadn't had before. This time they would not be victims of their own arrogance and deluded sense of invincibility. The Sol'agath witches were being disarmed.

"You can have a new man every day if you choose, Kate," Kevin said to appease the impetuous young sorceress. "But you'll have no more need for college courses."

"Cool." Kate snarled, a manifestation of the bloodlust that had empowered the Dor'chacht clan's malignant magic.

"But first we have to win," Kevin added, turning back to Karen. "I worked through the dinner rush tonight so Doug wouldn't think anything was wrong, just in case I have to go back to the shelter tomorrow to tag Paige."

"Wouldn't that be cutting it a little close?" Karen asked. "Besides, what if she calls in sick again?"

"I went to Paige's office to make the second contact yesterday, so that's out," Kevin said. "I'm open to other ideas, though."

"Why don't you just drop by their house tonight too?" Kate suggested.

"Wouldn't both of you dropping by be a little too obvious?" Karen asked.

"So what?" Kate shrugged. "After they're zapped, they'll be way too messed up to hurt us."

That's probably an accurate assessment, Kevin realized. The second contact with the artifacts had reduced the Charmed Ones' power levels to fifty percent. The third touch would drain another twenty-five percent, the most the witches could lose and retain enough magic to satisfy the rules of engagement. Anything less than a quarter of their powers and the Charmed Ones would be too human for the plan to proceed.

"All right," Kevin agreed. "I'll go by the house, but let's make sure we don't show up at the same time."

"Stuart is picking me up around nine thirty, so you've got plenty of time to get there first." Kate's blue eyes gleamed with cruel delight as she studied the gold band on her arm. Half of the engraved pattern had turned red, indicating that it contained half of Phoebe's magic.

Karen opened the wooden case and stared at her flute. As with Kate's bracelet and Kevin's cane, half the etched design on the instrument had turned red. She snapped the case closed. "I've got to get going. The guys will wonder what's going on if I don't get to P3 on time, and I don't want to answer any questions."

"With a Vengeance." Kate grinned. "Great name for a band, and the guys are cute, too. I vote to keep them around when this is over."

"Oh, I intend to." Karen stood up. "At least until they get boring and I decide to replace them. I'm not giving up my music just because I'll be able to make anyone do whatever I want anytime I want just by thinking about it."

"Man, I can relate. I can't wait to terrorize humans again." Kate sighed wistfully.

Kevin knew exactly how they felt. He missed his ability to change the physical properties of beings and things as much as Karen missed being able to inflict her will on any creature with a brain. Kate's power to command the elements was less elegant, but just as powerful.

"There's no thrill quite like hunting intelligent prey that's threatened by a force-five tornado," Kate added.

"Except maybe for vengeance," Kevin said softly.

During a dinner of miscellaneous Chinese dishes served on paper plates from paper containers, Piper had written down everything she and her sisters had done since Sunday. Leo's theory that they had all come in contact with something unusual twice in the past few days made sense, but the list had not produced anything helpful. Fresh out of tears following a prolonged crying jag over Leo's latest sudden departure, she sniffled in dismay.

"Are you sure you want me to add these two together?" Paige hesitated before dumping one half-full carton of leftovers into another. "I don't know about Leo, but I hate soggy chow mein noodles. They're supposed to be crisp."

"Whatever you think, Paige." A gurgling noise caught Piper's attention. She glanced toward the sink just as the gremlin jumped onto the counter. "Uh-oh!"

"What's that?" Phoebe wrinkled her nose in disgust.

Gilbert sniffed, then gurgled again. His mouth opened to reveal two rows of tiny, sharp teeth. Wiggling with excitement, he made a chattering sound that reminded Piper of an annoyed squirrel.

"A gremlin that's worn out his welcome." Paige grabbed a wooden spoon from a holder and took a step toward the bold frog creature.

"No!" Piper jumped up and pulled Paige back. "We've got to catch it, not hurt it. Remember?"

Phoebe typed with one wary eye on the agitated gremlin.

"Oh, yeah." Paige scowled. "Any ideas how? Because I'm not touching it."

"Don't look at me!" Piper shuddered at the thought.

"Oh, gross!" Phoebe gagged. "What does it want?"

Piper shrugged. "Chinese?"

Gilbert caught the fortune cookie Piper tossed and dove back into the garbage disposal.

Paige threw up her hands. "If you keep feeding it, we'll never get rid of it!"

"If we know where Gilbert is," Piper said, "maybe Cole can take care of it when he gets back. Since gremlins are indigenous to the underworld, upper-level demons must have some way to control them."

"There's never an ex-demon around when you need one," Paige quipped.

"Cole's expertise in the underworld comes in handy a lot, doesn't it?" Phoebe asked as though looking for confirmation.

"Yeah, it does." Paige nodded, smiling.

Gilbert is not our biggest problem right now, though, Piper thought as she sat back down. She picked up a pencil and scanned her notes.

If not for the Charmed factor that ruled their lives, their schedules would look completely ordinary and boring. Paige had been to work, the Fifth Street Shelter, and home. Phoebe had been to class and home, and Piper had been at P3 or home with only two exceptions: stopping for gas and getting money orders at the bank. She had finally agreed to let Leo grocery shop and run the other household errands.

"You were right, Paige," Piper said, bracing her forehead with her hand. "The only place we've all been this week that's the same is here."

"Maybe we forgot something." Paige carried three containers to the refrigerator and set them on a shelf beside Leo's double order of egg rolls and crab Rangoon.

"I'm sure I did." Phoebe clamped her pen between her teeth and flipped through the loose-leaf notebook she had used in her computer class.

No matter how bad things get, Piper thought with affection, *Phoebe always rallies.*

At the moment, Phoebe was acting on two of Paige's brilliant suggestions: She had made a paper copy of her list to carry in a pocket, and she was looking for hints about her recent activities in her class notes. Finding nothing in the notebook, she moved on to the papers she had taken out of her shoulder bag.

"Phoebe's got a point there," Paige said as she returned to the table. "She doesn't remember anything, and we don't *know* where she's been. We're just guessing."

"I went to Compute-A-Cup Monday night." Phoebe held up a credit card receipt. "I also paid for two coffees and two cheesecakes."

Piper penciled in the popular off-campus coffeehouse. "I don't suppose you know who you went with."

Paige glanced at Piper. "She picked up the tab, so it wasn't a guy."

"No way!" Phoebe's eyes blazed with indignation. "I love Cole. I don't have coffee with other guys just because he's out of town."

Piper glanced up. "What's the last thing you remember about Cole, Phoebe?"

"Kissing him good-bye." Phoebe frowned, looking sideways at Paige. "And talking about his trip at breakfast."

"That was Monday morning." Piper turned the top page and jotted the info on a blank sheet. "What else do you remember about Monday?"

"Not much." Phoebe nibbled her pencil eraser for a moment, thinking. "I did some ironing, had a sandwich for dinner with Leo 'cause you were at the club and Paige was at the shelter, and went to class."

"Is that where the blur starts?" Piper pressed. "In class?"

"Actually, now that you mention it—" The phone rang, interrupting Phoebe.

Paige picked up. "Halliwell house." After a moment she shoved the phone at Piper. "P3. Sounds important."

"This is Piper." Piper couldn't stem a new tide of frustrated tears as she listened to Dixie's panicked report. With a Vengeance had played a fantastic first set. The crowd loved them, but when Karen found out that Piper wasn't coming in, she had demanded immediate payment. No money, no second set . . . or third or fourth, either.

"Trouble?" Phoebe asked when Piper hung up.

"Musicians. Same thing." Piper paused to inhale and totally lost control when the doorbell rang. "Now what?" She asked through gulps of air between sobs.

"I'll find out." Paige rose and gripped Piper's shoulders. "Relax."

"Relax? I can't relax." Piper watched Paige disappear into the hall through misty eyes. She snatched her bag off the counter, threw it over her shoulder, and stomped after her. "I've got to go down to the club and pay the band before they walk and completely destroy P3's rep."

"What's their problem?" Phoebe ripped the memory list page off her yellow pad, folded it, and stuffed it with the pen into the front pocket of her jeans.

"Me, when I get there." Piper's fury smoldered in spite of the tears.

Piper slowed to collect herself when Paige opened the front door. She didn't recognize the blond man who carried a cane, and didn't feel like making excuses for her distress to a total stranger. He was not a stranger to Paige, though.

"Kevin!" Paige sounded pleasantly surprised. "What are you doing here?"

"Doug said you were sick, and, well—I was worried." Kevin leaned against the doorjamb. "I just thought I'd stop by to see if you need anything."

"Thanks, but I'll be fine after a good night's sleep." Paige held on to the doorknob, making no move to invite him in. "The extra hours at the shelter on top of my job just finally caught up with me."

Volunteers are coming in new and improved packaging these days, Piper thought as she smoothed back her hair and started toward the door. Considering Kevin's good looks and concerned interest, it wasn't a mystery why Paige had decided to work another week at the Fifth Street Shelter.

Kevin seemed startled to see Piper, which threw him off balance. As he pitched forward, the end of his cane flipped up and touched Paige's arm.

Piper caught a glimpse of the engraved design that began on the cane's silver handle and tapered off in the wooden shaft. Just as she realized it resembled the scrolling pattern on Karen's flute, Paige collapsed.

"Paige!" Piper's bag slipped down her arm as she broke her sister's fall.

"Hey, buddy!" Phoebe yelled from the kitchen doorway.

"Huh? I, uh—" Kevin held on to the door-jamb to steady himself while he planted the cane on the floor. He stared down at Paige for a stunned second, then glanced at Piper with a puzzled and worried look. "What's wrong with her?"

Piper eased her arm out from under Paige and let her bag drop. She wasn't exactly sure what had just happened, but it had to be related to Paige's sudden need for naps. One thing was certain: She didn't want Kevin hanging around complicating things with questions she couldn't answer.

"She's got, uh . . . narcolepsy," Piper said as Phoebe stormed toward the door. That wasn't exactly a lie considering Paige's unexplained condition.

"What's that?" Kevin asked anxiously, taking a step back.

"A sleep disorder," Piper explained. "People who have it fall asleep a lot"—she snapped her fingers—"just like that."

"Why did this bozo hit Paige with his cane?" Phoebe glared at Kevin.

"It was an accident," Kevin stammered. "I didn't—"

"Not your fault, Kevin." Piper cut him off. "I'll have Paige call you later, Kevin, but it would probably be better if you left now and let us handle things."

"Sure. I'll be at the shelter again tomorrow." With a tight smile, Kevin turned and hobbled down the steps.

Phoebe stepped into the open doorway. "Who was that guy?"

"One of the volunteers at the Fifth Street Shelter." Piper stooped beside her fallen sister.

Phoebe dropped to one knee. "What happened to her?"

Paige's breathing was slow and even. She snored softly.

"She fell asleep," Piper said.

"In the hall?" Phoebe looked at her askance, reflecting the same sense of bewilderment Piper felt. "Why?"

"Good question that I don't have time to answer right now." Piper shook Paige's shoulder. Paige swatted her hand away, but she didn't show any signs of waking up.

"Maybe we should move her to the couch, where she'll be more comfortable," Phoebe suggested.

"We can try." Piper gripped Paige under the arms. "Too bad she can't sleep orb."

"Like sleepwalk?" Phoebe grabbed Paige's ankles. "That would be a neat trick—"

"Oh, my," a woman said. "Is this a bad time, Phoebe?"

"Uh . . . sort of." Phoebe dropped Paige's feet and turned toward the woman standing on the front porch. "Do I know you?"

Piper eyed the new stranger's blonde hair and big baby blues with curiosity. The beautiful woman had the same physical characteristics as Kevin.

"You are such a riot!" The woman laughed and rolled her eyes. "Kate Dustin from your computer class? We had coffee together the other night at Compute-A-Cup?"

Piper stared. Karen Ashley in the substitute band was gorgeous with blonde hair, blue eyes, and perfect skin too. An uneasy feeling stirred in the pit of her stomach. For the Charmed Ones, there was no such thing as coincidence.

"Oh, yeah." Phoebe nodded, but she obviously didn't remember the woman. "And you're here because . . . ?"

Kate held out a spiral notebook. "Since you didn't make it to class tonight, I thought you could use my notes."

As Phoebe started to rise, Kate leaned over. When they bumped into each other, the notebook slipped from Kate's grasp.

"I'm such a klutz!" Kate exclaimed, bending to pick up the notebook at the same time Phoebe did. Her metal bracelet snagged on the loosely crocheted sleeve of Phoebe's sweater and pressed into Phoebe's arm as Kate carefully tried to untangle it. "Sorry about this."

Piper noticed the engraved pattern on the bracelet as Kate pulled it free. It was similar to the designs on Kevin's cane and Karen's flute, and most of it was red.

"That's okay . . ." Phoebe swayed slightly, as though she was about to faint.

Piper let go of Paige's arms to steady Phoebe. *Did touching Kate's bracelet trigger a vision?* she wondered.

Paige's head hit the floor, but she didn't wake up.

Kate frowned, perplexed by Phoebe's blank stare. "Is she all right?"

"Does she look all right?" Piper snapped. Things were happening too fast to figure out on the fly, but her initial uneasiness about Kate intensified.

"Hey, I was just trying to do Phoebe a favor." Kate raised her hands in a back-off gesture. She quickly retrieved the notebook, clutched it to her chest, and muttered as she turned to leave. "Forget it. What do I care if she flunks?"

"Who's that?" Phoebe peered over Piper's shoulder at Kate's receding back.

"That's Kate." Piper slammed the door closed. "I guess it's silly to hope you remember the vision you just got from her."

"I had a vision?" Phoebe asked. "Just now?"

"Not a clue, huh?" Piper sighed.

"Sorry." Phoebe winced with an apologetic shrug. "It was probably critically important, too, right?"

"Your premonitions usually are." Piper paused. She had assumed Phoebe was having a vision, but what if she had just gotten dizzy? That possibility triggered something she had overlooked as inconsequential. She had suffered temporary bouts of light-headedness immediately after touching Karen's flute . . . twice.

"Uh . . . Piper?" Phoebe tapped her on the shoulder. "There's a strange lady sleeping in our hall."

"Oh, that's just great!" Piper threw up her hands. "Please, don't tell me you've forgotten who Paige is."

"Paige." Phoebe smiled tightly. "Can you give me a hint?"

"What's the last thing you remember?" Piper asked, frantic.

Phoebe frowned. "Cole killed a witch, only he didn't really, because he was tricked by some guy in the Brotherhood of Thorn."

Piper's eyes widened with disbelief. Phoebe was relating events that had happened months ago!

"But then I became a banshee," Phoebe rambled on, smiling suddenly. "And I found out that Cole really loves me and I love him. There's a way to work this out, Piper. I couldn't possibly love Cole if he was evil. I couldn't."

"We are in so much trouble." Piper sagged against the wall.

"I can't drink another cup of coffee!" Paige covered her mouth to make the point. Piper's caffeine cure for acute fatigue was working to some extent, but her stomach was rebelling.

"Okay, but don't you dare fall asleep." Sniffling, Piper picked up the phone when it rang and whined, "Now what, Dixie?"

There isn't even a partially effective cure for Piper's nonstop blubbering, Paige thought, which was too bad. Chronic glee had been a lot easier to live with.

Forgetting her own power deficiency problem, Paige tried to orb her empty cup into the sink. When the orb particles finally arrived, a pile of china shards materialized instead of the cup. She orbed those into the trash, which seemed to take forever.

Sighing, Paige glanced at Phoebe's laptop screen. The middle Halliwell sister wasn't faring a whole lot better than her older and younger siblings. In addition to the total lack of short-term recall, Phoebe had developed a huge gap in her long-term memory. She had forgotten everything that had happened since just before Prue had been killed.

Phoebe hit "save" and picked up her pen to update the paper cheat sheets she kept in her pocket. She scanned her reference notes, then looked up with a sober expression. "Paige, right?"

"Right." Paige just nodded. She and Piper had tried to fill in the more important events in Phoebe's missing memory. Finding out that the Source was vanquished, Cole was human, and they were engaged had only slightly softened the shock and pain of Prue's death.

"I can't come in tonight, Dixie," Piper said. "Karen will just have to wait until tomorrow." Piper punched the phone off and dabbed her eyes with a paper napkin. "Now she wants to be paid in advance for the whole gig."

"Which translates as, 'I want to get to Piper,'" Paige said. When it had become obvious that her exhaustion and Phoebe's memory were worse after visits from Kevin Graves and Kate Dustin, they had finally begun connecting dots.

Aside from the similarity in appearance, Kevin and Kate had both first met her and Phoebe on Monday, just like Karen and Piper. Then Piper had realized that no serious, ambitious band would tolerate Karen's temperamental fit about money.

According to Dixie, the demand for payment had come *after* Karen learned that Piper wasn't going to the club. Considering that Kevin and Kate had both concocted excuses to visit the house, risking exposure in order to contact Phoebe and herself, only one conclusion could be drawn. Karen's actions were a desperate attempt to lure Piper to P3. To avoid walking into a possible trap, Piper had authorized Dixie to pay With a Vengeance from the cash register after each set.

"Where is Leo?" Piper looked up, pleading. "Can't you guys speed things up a little?"

Piper's raised voice jerked Paige back from nodding off. "I've got to do something to stay awake. Something caffeine free."

"Let's go over everything I've written down to make sure I've got it straight." Phoebe braced a foot on the edge of her chair, pen poised over her pad. "Kevin, Karen, and Kate are using a cane, a flute, and a bracelet to steal our powers."

"That's what it looks like," Piper said.

As much as Paige didn't want to believe Kevin was a bad guy, no other explanation made sense. He had touched her with the cane three times: Monday at the shelter, Wednesday at the clinic, and tonight. Her fatigue had been greater and her powers weaker after each encounter.

"And we're how sure of this?" Phoebe looked from one sister to the other.

"Pretty sure." Paige stood up and began to pace. The movement helped ward off the sleepiness. "Earlier you seemed to think your memory losses started when your Web site class did. Kate was there Monday night, and Piper heard her say that she went with you for coffee."

"She was in class with you last night, too,"
Piper added. "I called and caught Professor
Deekle before he left his office tonight, and he
confirmed it. She sat directly behind you."

"Which gave her plenty of opportunity to
touch you with her bracelet," Paige said as she
walked circles around the stove island.

"Yeah, I got that." Phoebe chewed on the end
of the pen as she studied her paper. "Funny
thing, though."

Piper pulled another tissue from the box on the
table and blew her nose. "I fail to see the humor."

"I meant how the songs Karen played dic-
tated your mood changes. I remember something like that," Phoebe explained, "from a
paper I did back in high school."

"You're kidding." Paige stopped pacing to
stare.

"No. Weird, huh?" Phoebe leaned forward,
rushing her words before she forgot what she
wanted to say. "There was this Tuatha de
Danann guy in ancient Ireland called Dagda.
He had a harp that manipulated emotions."

"What's a Tuatha de Danann?" Paige asked.

"Magic people who lived on the island before
the Celts arrived in roughly one thousand B.C.,"
Phoebe said. "According to the legends, the
Danann went underground. All the modern Irish
myths are derivatives of that ancient culture."

"What did we have for dinner, Phoebe?"
Piper asked.

"Uh . . . don't know." Phoebe sighed.

Paige blinked. "Why is it that you don't know what we had for dinner but you can remember all that historical stuff?"

"All what historical stuff?" Phoebe's gaze shifted as Leo appeared in swirls of sparkling light. "Hey, Leo!"

Piper rose and threw her arms around Leo's neck. Tears rolled down her cheeks. "It's about time you showed up."

"The Elders' archives are pretty extensive," Leo said. "How are things here?"

"That might take a while to explain." Piper patted his shoulder. "Hungry?"

While Piper heated Leo's dinner in the microwave, Paige paced and gave him the encapsulated version of their findings. He was up to speed by the time Piper placed a plate of steaming egg rolls, crab Rangoon, and chow mein mixed with limp noodles in front of him.

"So you were right, Leo." Paige sank back into a chair. The weariness was fast becoming too hard to fight off. "We *were* all exposed to something—or rather, someone."

"Both, actually," Piper said. "The evil Ks and their engraved artifacts. I don't know if this means anything, but part of the designs on the bracelet and cane were red. There was no red on Karen's flute Monday, but there was yesterday."

Leo finished chewing a bite of chow mein and swallowed. "The red could be a measure of the amount of power the artifacts have absorbed. How much of the designs were red?"

Piper squinted, thinking. "Roughly three quarters on the cane and bracelet. One quarter on the flute, but that was before she hit me with the weeping whammy."

"But why drain our magic slowly?" Paige asked. "Why not just zap all our powers at once, like the demons who were possessed by the Hollow did?"

"The hollow what?" Phoebe positioned her fingers over the laptop keyboard to type.

She isn't trying to be funny, Paige realized. Phoebe didn't remember the ultimate power that consumed all magic, because they had encountered it too recently.

"It's only relevant as an example, Phoebe." Piper looked back at Leo. "So why not just zap our powers dry?"

"Because then you'd be mortals, and the Higher Powers could negate any magic used against you." Leo put down his fork. "It's kind of like the 'no magic for personal gain' rule."

"Wait a minute," Paige said. "Evil uses magic against innocents all the time."

"Yes, but there are rules of engagement for magical feuds," Leo explained. "Break them and forfeit."

"Sounds like this trip to the great above wasn't a waste of time," Piper said.

"Not completely." Leo pushed his plate aside and folded his arms. "It took some digging, but the Elders found an obscure reference to the warriors of darkness and champions of virtue—"

Paige snapped her head up. Leo was still talking, but she had obviously dozed off.

"—duel between the magical clans of the Sol'agath and the Dor'chacht. It was a classic example of good versus evil."

"The who and the what?" Phoebe did a double take.

"That didn't ring a bell with me, either," Piper said.

"I missed it too." Paige propped her chin to listen and pinched her leg to stay awake.

Leo patiently repeated himself. "The Sol'agath and Dor'chacht were ancient clans that coexisted on Earth—until the Dor'chacht decided to challenge the Sol'agath for magical supremacy in the mortal realm three thousand years ago."

"The warriors of darkness were the bad guys, right?" Phoebe began typing, anticipating the answer.

"Yes," Leo said. "The Sol'agath were your ancestors."

"We go that far back?" Piper was stunned.

"Melinda Warren wasn't the beginning, then?" Phoebe grinned, pleased that she had remembered a significant part of the family history.

"Melinda was the beginning of the Charmed cycle." Leo snatched the last crab Rangoon off the plate as Piper reached for it. "Sorry, Piper, but I *really* like crab Rangoon."

"I thought you were done," Piper whined. She brushed away a tear and picked up the last egg roll.

"Okay, so the Dor'chacht clan challenged the Sol'agath clan three thousand years ago," Phoebe read off her computer screen. "What happened?"

"The Sol'agath won," Leo said, "and their descendants have lived among humans using magic to do good ever since. If they had lost, they could have chosen between ascending to a higher plane of benevolent existence or becoming mortal."

"But the Dor'chacht lost." Piper frowned. "So what happened to them?"

Leo held up a hand while he finished off the crab Rangoon. "Since they were empowered by evil, they should have forfeited human form and been banished to the underworld."

"But?" Phoebe prompted.

"But if the portent of the poem you found in *The Book of Shadows* is correct," Leo continued, "then apparently some of the Dor'chacht have survived . . . in human form."

"What does that mean to us?" Piper asked.

"I don't know." Leo looked worried. "Nobody from the Dor'chacht clan should be here!"

"But they are." Paige frowned, wishing she

hadn't returned *The Book of Shadows* to the attic before dinner. She thought about walking upstairs to read the poem again, but she didn't have the energy. "Didn't the verse say that the champions of virtue had to defend the 'light of ages' or be forsaken, like the warriors of darkness were before?"

"A rematch?" Phoebe offered.

"Makes sense," Paige agreed, yawning, "but it's just an assumption."

"Except if some of the Dor'chacht survived," Leo said, "then technically the original battle never ended."

"Is that a major or a minor distinction?" Paige had learned that the smallest detail sometimes made the biggest difference when dealing with magical adversaries.

"Well, it could mean that the Dor'chacht haven't lost yet . . . exactly." Leo shrugged. "And if they didn't lose, then it's possible they wouldn't have been forced into the underworld."

"Okay, but if that's true, where did they go?" Anger flashed in Piper's teary eyes. "We aren't up against the whole Dor'chacht clan, are we?"

"No," Leo said with conviction. "In matters of great consequence, the forces of good and evil must be balanced. Whoever cast the spell back then knew that. Whatever's going on, I'm sure it's three on three. The rest of the Dor'chacht clan may be suspended in time and space, waiting for their ultimate fate to be decided."

"Wouldn't the higher powers have known that they slipped away?" Paige asked.

"Not necessarily," Leo explained. "They can't detect suspended magic or track what's going on in the underworld. Just like I can't sense any of you down there."

"Sounds to me like we're just guessing," Phoebe said.

"We are." Piper's eyes narrowed. "But I know someone who has the answers."

"Karen," Leo said.

"Who just can't wait to zap Piper with her magic flute." To keep from dozing off, Paige stood and reached for Leo's plate. The only thing left was a small mound of cold chow mein on noodles long past a state of tasty crunch. "Are you done with this now?"

Leo nodded, but he was focused on Piper. "You can't risk a confrontation with her, Piper."

"I can if all of you are there to back me up." Piper's eyes welled with tears and her voice shook, but there was no doubting her determination. "Karen stole *some* of my power, not all of it."

"Fifty percent," Leo clarified. "Assuming one quarter of red in the patterns represents one contact."

Piper touched the flute twice, so Leo's math makes perfect sense, Paige thought as she carried the plate

to the sink. The pile of garbage on the disposal side
was only half the size it had been earlier. Gilbert
wasn't as fast or efficient as the mechanical
garbage disposal, but he was making progress.

Phoebe used the laptop trackball to scroll,
then looked up. "Unless my notes are incomplete, the artifacts are the *only* magic they've
used on us. As long as Piper doesn't touch the
flute, she should be safe."

"But we can't rely on my power to keep that
from happening. If I tried to orb the flute, it would
probably turn into sawdust," Paige said. The
destructive quality of her faulty power might come
in handy at some point, but not in this instance.

Piper was quick to agree. "Definitely not a
good idea."

"Why not?" Phoebe asked. "Wouldn't that stop
Karen from stealing more of Piper's powers?"

"Yeah, but as far as we know, our powers are
being stored in the artifacts," Paige explained as she
added the chow mein to the rest of Gilbert's chow.

"And destroying them might send our
powers into the void," Phoebe finished with a
frustrated sigh. "That's a keeper." She typed
the information into her computer file, then
scribbled a notation on her papers.

Piper shot out of her chair. "I want my powers and some answers, and there's only one
place to get them."

"There's no guarantee Karen will tell you
anything," Leo said.

"She's gone to a lot of trouble to get me to P3 tonight," Piper said, refusing to be deterred. "And I'm not going to disappoint her. Do we drive or orb over?"

Phoebe stuffed her paper notes in her pocket, closed the laptop, and tucked it under her arm. "Orbing is faster."

"Fine, but since Kevin drained my powers, Leo will have to orb all of us." Paige turned on the water to rinse off the plate and stepped back when Gilbert's pliable body oozed out of the tap.

The gremlin hissed, spraying Paige with underworld rodent slime. She gagged as the screeching creature dove into the pile of garbage and burrowed back into the disposal.

"I can orb you into mush, you know!" Paige glared into the sink.

Gilbert thrust his head up and spit out a wad of chow mein noodles.

Paige glanced at her family with a resigned sigh.

"Life doesn't get a whole lot more interesting than this, does it?"

Chapter 7

Phoebe gasped as her body dissolved into a stream of photon particles. Her consciousness seemed to meld with the vastness of the cosmos for an instant before she re-formed in the alley behind P3, clinging to Leo, Piper, and her newly discovered half sister, Paige. The tingling she felt in every cell dissipated with the orb sparkles.

"That is such a rush!" Phoebe exclaimed.

"And scary until you get used to it." Paige slouched against the Dumpster and smothered a yawn with her hand.

"You can orb from one place to another?" Phoebe asked with a nervous glance around the dark alley. "What are we doing here?"

"We don't have time to explain, Phoebe," Piper said. Her eyes were red from crying. She pulled keys out of her bag and unlocked the delivery door into the club. "Check the laptop under your arm or the notes in your pocket. Better yet, just do whatever we tell you."

Leo glanced at his watch. "Dixie should have given last call five minutes ago."

Phoebe saw that Paige was wearing high boots, a short skirt, and a stylish blouse with billowing long sleeves. Piper's long skirt, scoop-neck top, and ankle boots were casually classy. She, however, was dressed in jeans, sneakers, and a faded U2 T-shirt. *Apparently, we aren't going to P3 to socialize,* she thought.

Piper held the door open as Paige and Leo ducked inside. Phoebe followed Piper, who motioned everyone into the storeroom.

Paige sat down on a reinforced cardboard box full of stemware. She looked exhausted. "Do we have a plan?"

"We have a general idea," Piper said. "That'll have to do."

Phoebe almost asked what dire danger they had gotten themselves into now, but Piper looked so upset, she decided to just go with the flow. She set the compact computer on a stack of cardboard boxes, turned it on, and opened the last file she had been using.

Piper dialed her cell phone. "Dixie. It's Piper. Tell me exactly how things stand in the bar. I mean, right now, this minute."

Leo stood watch at the door while Paige caught some Zs. Piper just kept nodding with her ear to her cell phone. In the dark about everything, Phoebe took the opportunity to glance at the detailed notes in the computer file.

It only took her a minute to realize that her memory—short- and long-term—was completely unreliable, thanks to a power-draining bracelet wielded by someone named Kate. Since she couldn't trust herself to make appropriate decisions, the only sensible thing to do was to take Piper's advice and follow orders. She took out of her pocket the pen and paper notes mentioned on the laptop.

"Okay, here's what I want you to do, Dixie." Piper kept her voice low. "Get rid of the last few customers and the band, except for Karen. Tell her I'll be there shortly to take care of her. Then lock up and go home."

Phoebe folded her paper notes so the visible portion was blank. Then she wrote, "Don't ask, just do whatever Piper and Paige say. Important!"

Piper paused. "You already used tonight's cash to pay her, Dixie, so there's no money in the register to steal. Just call my cell as soon as you're out of there—in two minutes or less, if possible, please."

"Is it smart to warn Karen that you're coming?" Leo asked, worried.

"Probably not, but we have to talk to her alone," Piper explained. "We can't risk having any innocents caught in the middle, especially since our magic is messed up. Besides, I doubt Karen expects all of us to pop out of the storeroom in a couple minutes."

"I'm ready for"—Phoebe drew a blank—"whatever."

A thud sounded behind her, and Piper's eyes widened in alarm. Phoebe turned as Paige curled up on the floor. Falling off the carton had not disturbed her deep slumber.

"Wake Paige up, Leo, and try to keep her awake, please." Piper glared at her phone. "Come on, Dixie . . ." She punched the talk button when the ringer sounded. "Dixie. Great. Thanks. I'll see you tomorrow."

"Did we come up with a plan, yet?" Paige wobbled as Leo helped her to her feet.

"We're going to bluff and hope our mental prowess is as effective as our magical powers used to be." Piper stuffed the phone into her bag.

"Well, brains can usually beat out muscle," Paige said. "So why not magic, too?"

Phoebe couldn't type or read fast enough to keep up with everything. Since the paper in her hand said it was important to obey Piper, she decided to just take her own advice. Leaving the laptop behind, she palmed her paper notes and followed Paige, Leo, and Piper into the bar. A blonde woman sat on the edge of a small stage.

"Piper." The woman spoke with deadly calm. "Who're your friends?"

"They're family, actually." Piper folded her arms, ignoring a solitary tear that traced a slow path down the side of her face. "Let's just skip the small talk and get right to the heart of our issues, Karen."

"Certainly." Karen reached for a wooden flute lying on the stage behind her.

"Forget it." Piper's tone was cutting in spite of her sobs. "I'm not touching your flute."

"So you figured it out." Karen set the flute in her lap and shrugged. "There's nothing you can do now, though. Your powers are useless."

"Not completely." Paige held out her hand and glanced toward the bar. "Candle!"

Phoebe tensed as a teardrop candle turned into a burst of flickering light. However, when it reappeared in Paige's hand, it was a mass of melted glass and shredded wax.

"Was that a threat?" Karen asked, unruffled.

"A reminder," Paige said. "We're not helpless."

"Nice try, but I'm one hundred percent human. No powers." Karen smiled. "You can't use magic on me without suffering the consequences."

"She's right," Leo said. "That's why Karen, Kevin, and Kate haven't stolen *all* your powers, remember? They can't challenge mortals, and neither can you."

"But they won't be mortal when we finish fighting our family feud, will you?" Piper's question was phrased as a statement of fact. She held Karen's gaze as she pulled out a chair and sat down.

What feud? Phoebe scanned her notes until she found references to an ancient battle between two magical clans called the Sol'agath and Dor'chacht. As she reviewed what little they knew, she realized Piper was pretending to know more than she actually did, hoping Karen could be tricked into giving them specific information.

"Why would I tell you anything?" Karen scoffed.

Paige took a chair beside Piper and flexed her fingers. "Because you can't be absolutely certain that I'll honor the rules. I haven't been in the good-witch business as long as my sisters."

"Paige was an incredibly powerful, extremely evil enchantress in a previous life," Piper added. "She hasn't even begun to tap her magical resources in *this* life."

"You're bluffing," Karen said.

Due to her missing memories of the past several months, Phoebe had only known Paige a few hours. However, since she had been evil in a past life too, she knew that Paige could not possibly be evil and still be a Charmed One now. Piper was gambling that *Karen* didn't know that.

"Maybe." Piper's sniffles didn't dampen the

chilling effect of her unwavering stare. "If you'd rather not find out, I suggest you start talking."

As she sat down at the next table, Phoebe noted a flicker of doubt in the blonde woman's eyes. Piper's ploy to rattle her was working.

Karen hesitated, then shrugged. "All right. You can't thwart our destiny this time, so what harm can it do?"

"This time?" Phoebe glanced toward Piper.

"Our ancestors beat the Dor'chacht in a fight three thousand years ago," Piper explained, "but they didn't like losing."

"So they're looking for a rematch," Paige added.

Karen inhaled sharply, apparently shocked at how much Phoebe's sisters had deduced. She recovered quickly. "Yes. Shen'arch arranged it before the Sol'agath struck the winning blow."

Since it was all news to Phoebe, the suspense had her on the edge of her seat.

"Shen'arch?" Leo asked.

"Chief sorcerer of the Dor'chacht clan," Karen offered proudly. "The greatest master of magic that ever walked the Earth."

"He couldn't have been *that* great," Paige said. "He's not here."

Karen smiled. "He will be, after we reclaim the destiny your Sol'agath ancestors stole from us. Then we'll become the dominant magical force in the mortal world."

"Their ancestors won fair and square," Leo

said tightly. "That fact doesn't change just because Shen'arch figured out how to beat the system."

"Bureaucracy must be a universal constant," Paige murmured as she started to doze off.

"How did Shen'arch do that?" Piper asked.

Phoebe realized that Piper was counting on Karen's eagerness to brag about her ancient leader's prowess to reveal something useful. A moment later, she had no idea who Karen was talking about.

"Shen'arch transferred the powers of the Dor'chacht's best warriors into objects so the Higher Powers couldn't find them," Karen said.

Phoebe frowned. "So they couldn't find the powers or the warriors?"

"The powers." Karen gripped the flute tighter.

"That's why the Elders didn't know anything." Leo paled as the seriousness of the situation began to sink in. "There was no magical signature to track."

"Not for the past three thousand years." Karen gloated. She was enjoying the discomfort her disclosures caused the Charmed descendants of her enemies. "And as long as the Dor'chacht magic is not released until the battle is rejoined, the Higher Powers cannot touch us."

"How convenient," Piper said.

"You're one of the warriors?" Phoebe asked.

"I am Sh'tara, the mind-bender." Karen's posture stiffened, her blue eyes narrowed to piercing slits, and her mouth curled into a sneer. "The warrior essences of Tov'reh, Ce'kahn, and myself were transferred into three humans at the instant of conception, twenty-six years ago."

Paige opened one eye. "Kevin, Kate, and you."

"In that order, yes." Karen's satisfied smile was cold, her gaze devoid of human compassion.

Paige glared at Karen. "Okay, so this Shen'arch guy found a loophole, and the Dor'chacht get a second chance. What makes you so sure you can win this time?"

Piper rolled her eyes. "Because they're cheating."

"Nonsense. All's fair in matters of war." Karen laughed and held up her flute.

"By making your magic ineffectual instead of taking all your powers away," Leo said, "the Dor'chacht can challenge you to combat under the ancient rules of engagement without fear of reprisal." His gaze shifted from Piper to Paige and Phoebe. "But with your magic and the Power of Three diminished, a Dor'chacht victory is certain."

"Leo!" Piper glowered at her husband for daring to doubt the Charmed Ones' ability to overcome impossible odds.

"Time!" Paige jumped out of her chair and made a T with her hands. "I zoned out at 'second chance.' Can someone fill me in on what I missed?"

"I've said all I have to say." Karen stood up and placed the flute in its case. She snapped it closed and paused at the base of the stairs. "Until tomorrow, then."

"Tomorrow?" Piper scowled. "What about tomorrow?"

"You'll find out at midnight." Karen flipped her long hair over her shoulder and mounted the stairs with the unhurried step of someone in complete control. She unlocked the door and let it fall softly closed behind her.

Phoebe hadn't realized she was holding her breath until Karen was gone. She exhaled with a whoosh.

Piper cuffed Leo's arm. "Their victory is a certainty? What was *that* all about?"

"Yeah, that's what I'd like to know." Paige struggled to keep her eyes open. "Actually, I've got a bunch of blanks that need filling in."

"Can I get a soda from the bar?" Phoebe asked.

"Sure." Piper glanced at Leo and folded her arms. "Okay, mister, explain yourself."

"Arrogance may be the Dor'chacht's worst enemy," Leo said, "because they think they have an unbeatable edge."

"They do!" The torrential tears Piper had been keeping in check burst from her eyes. "Our powers are practically drained dry."

"They don't have their powers either," Paige said. "Not at the moment anyway."

"But we can't use the magic we have left

against them now because they're human and we're not." Piper blinked back more tears.

"A sorcerer as powerful and cunning as Shen'arch would leave nothing to chance." Leo shifted uncomfortably. "It's probably safe to assume the Dor'chacht can get their powers back without releasing yours when the battle begins."

"Tomorrow at midnight." Piper sighed.

"What if we don't show up?" Paige swayed to the side but caught herself before she toppled off the chair. "It takes two sides to wage a war."

"Except your only choice will be to fight or die." Leo shrugged, as though to apologize for ancient ritual codes he couldn't help or change. "In ancient times, all magical family disputes were settled in the Valley of Ages. Since tomorrow's battle is essentially a continuation of the original conflict, it will be held there too."

"So?" Phoebe leaned on the bar, sipping her soda. She didn't understand the problem. Nobody could fight somebody who wasn't there, like Paige said.

"So at midnight tomorrow," Leo said, "you'll all be automatically transported to the Valley of Ages to face the Dor'chacht clan's chosen three."

"I know I'm not going to like the answer, but I have to ask." Piper started to blow her nose, but her tissue fell apart. Fighting another rush of tears, she grabbed a stack of cocktail napkins off the bar. "What happens if we lose?"

All three witches focused on the Whitelighter.

Leo didn't try to cushion the blow. "You and anyone else who has Sol'agath blood will lose your powers . . . forever."

"And?" Paige rocked forward.

Feeling chilled, Phoebe rubbed her arms.

Leo sighed. "And since there will be no benevolent magic or Charmed Ones to protect the innocent, humanity will ultimately succumb to the influences of evil and embrace the darker side of human nature."

Chapter

8

Clutching the phone, Kevin sat up in bed and glanced at the time. It was almost three in the morning. Karen had called as soon as she had left P3 to tell him about her confrontation with the Charmed Ones.

"I wasn't able to drain the last portion of Piper's power," Karen stated flatly.

"Unfortunate, but not a disaster," Kevin assured her. It was long past the time anything could stop the mystical processes Shen'arch had set in motion millennia before. "It probably wouldn't hurt to have a strategy meeting tomorrow, though."

"Whatever, just as long as we succeed." Karen paused, as though savoring the thought she expressed. "You have no idea how anxious I am to command their Sol'agath minds."

"As much as Ce'kahn is looking forward to

whipping up a hurricane?" Kevin smiled, imagining Paige as a magnificent centaur. He could hardly wait until he was infused with his lost power to transform anything and anyone into whatever he desired. "Tomorrow, Sh'tara."

"Destiny awaits, Tov'reh."

After Karen hung up, Kevin was too restless to stay cooped up indoors. Stripped of his magical power, he had been condemned to live among ordinary humans as an ordinary human, and he had resented every minute of the past twenty-six years. Now, thanks to the quick thinking and cunning of the Dor'chacht's most powerful sorcerer, Shen'arch, they were only hours away from taking back what the Sol'agath had stolen from them.

Slipping into sweats, Kevin stepped outside the lower level garden apartment and paused to test scent. The damp musk of decomposing leaves and human sweat were overpowered by the repugnant odors of gasoline fumes and other unnatural chemical compounds. He gagged, then snorted to expel the foul industrial taints from his nostrils. The ultrasensitive senses he had inherited from his previous life as a warrior sorcerer had been hard to disguise while he was growing up in suburban Seattle. Soon he wouldn't have to care if his primitive inclinations might offend his more civilized contemporaries. They would be at his barbaric mercy.

The refined Sol'agath never should have beaten the savage Dor'chacht, Kevin thought as he ran across the street into the neighborhood park. A narrow strip of woods along the perimeter encircled a broad, manicured meadow. The artificial wilderness wasn't ideal, but it helped revive his spirit and settle his thoughts.

Moving with animal stealth, Kevin kept to the trees that paralleled the paths. Exercising prudence, he rarely indulged the hunter's instinct to stalk the few joggers whose high-pressure careers forced them to run at night or in the early morning. They never saw or heard him. It was a game he had played since childhood, a way to prove his superiority over the humans he loathed. He despised being one of them even more, a prisoner in his body, unable to alter his form or theirs.

But not for long, Kevin thought as he ran through the woods. He was alone in the darkness of the predawn hours, but he welcomed the solitude. Tomorrow he would be able to kill with a word.

Sitting on a bench, Kevin closed his eyes and let his mind drift back to the last, fateful minutes of his real life.

He had been soaring above the battlefield, his falcon's beak and talons dripping with Sol'agath blood. Then Shen'arch had pulled him out of the sky. . . .

• • •

Tov'reh could not fight the master sorcerer's enormous power or ignore Shen'arch's command to come. When his feet touched the rain-soaked earth, he stumbled as hooked talons reverted to feet wrapped in furs and leather thongs. Feathered wings and head plume became bruised flesh and matted hair. Exposed to the fury of Ce'kahn's storm and more vulnerable to the Sol'agath's magic in man form, he dove for cover behind a fallen tree.

Shen'arch was waiting, but Tov'reh would be of no use to the old man if he was vanquished by a spell or blackened into char by lightning.

"Tov'reh!" The sound of Sh'tara's panicked call reached him on a wave of rolling thunder. "Where are you?"

Tov'reh crawled to the end of the massive tree trunk and looked across the forbidding expanse of the Valley of Ages. Separated and concealed from the mortal realm by cosmic wards and impassable mountains, the valley had been the arena for magical blood feuds since the first chosen primals had learned to channel elemental power. Now, although enclaves of magical people were scattered around the globe, only two major clans remained: the Dor'chacht and the Sol'agath. Within the hour, there would be only one.

"Sh'tara!" Tov'reh stood up, watching anxiously as the mind-bender dashed around geysers of steam venting from fissures in the rocky valley floor.

On a high butte to her right, a pair of Sol'agath witches joined hands and began to recite. The words were lost in the howl of the wind, but that didn't diminish the effects of their spell. A tower of jagged rock erupted from the ground in front of Sh'tara and sprouted tendrils of molten ore. Sh'tara's power to command minds was useless against mindless rock. She hesitated as fingers of metal fire began to close around her.

"Ice!" Tov'reh focused on the molten rock formation, but his power was ebbing into the ether. He was not strong enough to negate the Sol'agath spell, but the burning trap froze long enough for Sh'tara to race beyond it.

As she ran toward him, it was obvious Sh'tara's energies were almost depleted. Tov'reh wished he could endow her with the powerful, swift legs of a horse, but he dared not sap any more of his strength. He swore when she stopped to retrieve the wooden flute that fell off her belt, but the Sol'agath witches on the butte had turned their attention and their magic on someone else.

"Shen'arch is calling," Sh'tara blurted out when she reached his side. "We must find Ce'kahn."

"I know." Tov'reh wrapped an arm around the breathless sorceress and scanned the valley behind him. During brief flashes of lightning, he caught glimpses of the raging battle obscured in the drizzle of Ce'kahn's waning storm.

Blond and blue-eyed, the Dor'chacht warriors wore metal armor inlaid with gold and silver over leather, furs, and tunics woven of coarse fabrics. The ferocious sorcerers hurled explosive spells and brandished enchanted swords against the dark-haired witches, who wore unadorned shirts, leggings, and robes. Peaceful by nature, the Sol'agath defended themselves with shields and spells that reflected the virulent evil of the Dor'chacht's destructive power. The molten rock tower had been conjured from the hardness of Sh'tara's heart and the smoldering embers of her seething but unshakable resolve.

And every successful Sol'agath spell diminished Dor'chacht power.

"There she is." Sh'tara pointed, shouting to be heard over the clang of sword against shield and the roar of Dor'chacht curses. "Over there."

Spotting Ce'kahn lying in a pool of mud, Tov'reh ran toward her with Sh'tara following behind. He was stricken with sudden despair when he saw Shen'arch approaching from the opposite direction. The master sorcerer rarely expended physical energies, preferring to rely on his magics. Since the old man was not using his powers to find them, the outcome of the battle seemed not to bode well for the Dor'chacht.

"Here. The tempest has tired you." Tov'reh extended his hand to help Ce'kahn rise, but she hissed to warn him back. When he did not move fast enough, her temper flared. A bolt of light-ning struck the ground at his feet.

"Enough bickering among yourselves!" Shen'arch swatted Ce'kahn's leg with his silver tipped staff. His scowl was dark, his mood foul. "Do you not feel your magic being drawn away? The battle is lost, and we are almost out of time."

"I will never surrender," Ce'kahn spat as she struggled to stand. Slashes of blood and mud streaked her cheeks and brow. Her long golden hair was tangled with twigs and black vines, and her cold blue eyes glinted with defiance.

Sh'tara threw her head back in a shriek of rage.

Tov'reh compressed his anger into a glare he fixed on the old sorcerer. "*We* challenged the Sol'agath, Shen'arch. If we lose, everyone in the clan will forfeit their power and magical identity forever."

"Yes, yes." The old man waved his staff with annoyed impatience. "But there is an exception to every supernatural law, Tov'reh, or so it often seems."

"Are you saying we can thwart fate?" Sh'tara asked, incredulous.

"If the bones read true," the sorcerer said, "the Dor'chacht have *one* chance to reverse des-tiny, to save later what we will lose now. We must act quickly, though."

"I'll do anything to prevent the Sol'agath from having magical dominance in the mortal world," Ce'kahn said.

Tov'reh and Sh'tara both nodded.

"We cannot prevent the Sol'agath from reaping the rewards of their victory," Shen'arch said, "but their reign does not have to last forever."

"Explain," Tov'reh demanded, intrigued.

"First we must hide your magics so the Higher Powers cannot steal them now or detect them in the future." Shen'arch placed his silver-tipped staff on the ground with Sh'tara's flute and one of Ce'kahn's gold armbands.

No one questioned the wisdom of the plan. When the master sorcerer instructed them to kneel with a hand on the objects, Tov'reh touched the wooden staff. At Shen'arch's command, he used his remaining power to transform the long pole into a shorter walking stick with a curved, silver handle.

Shen'arch raised his arms, his voice strong as he intoned his spell. "Dark magics of the Dor'chacht clan, all powers that were yours return; course through the blood, flow from the hand into these lifeless vessels burn!"

The blood in Tov'reh's veins grew hot as his power flooded back into him, then cooled as the recovered abilities rushed through his fingertips into the staff. Before he collapsed on the ground beside Sh'tara and Ce'kahn, he saw that all three artifacts had been etched with the scrolling symbols of infinite and eternal magic.

"Listen and remember," Shen'arch said.

Exhausted and weak, Tov'reh closed his eyes and drifted off under the hypnotic lull of Shen'arch's whispered words.

"You will sleep now and awaken in three times a thousand years. What must be known will be known at the proper time. Warriors of darkness, die now to live again. The fate of all goes with you. . . ."

Shaking himself from the reflective trance, Kevin brushed his hair back with both hands and took a deep breath. He still marveled at Shen'arch's wisdom and power.

Everything had happened just as the ancient sorcerer had predicted. Their spirits, memories, and personalities had been transferred from the ancient battlefield directly into new bodies twenty-six years shy of three millennia in the future.

Born into abandoned infants and adopted by different families, Kevin, Karen, and Kate had all been told what they had to do and needed to know in adolescent dreams. Driven by identical imperatives, they had all arrived in the same French village on the same day two years ago. They had recognized one another immediately and had had no trouble finding the cave where Shen'arch had stashed the flute, armband, and cane. However, to prevent the Higher Powers from discovering their Dor'chacht identity and taking their powers, they could not release the hidden magics until the vengeance battle began.

But we haven't spent the intervening time being idle, Kevin thought as he stood up and stretched. Knowing the difficulties they would face, the crafty old sorcerer had not been content with simply preserving their magic. The cosmic configurations that made a rematch possible would only happen once, against descendants of the Sol'agath who commanded an immense concentration of benevolent magic known as the Power of Three.

To counter this, the old man had stacked the magical deck in favor of the Dor'chacht clan's champions. Not only would Tov'reh, Ce'kahn, and Sh'tara have the full force of their own abilities when the duel commenced, the Sol'agath would have lost most of theirs.

Kevin smiled.

Even though Piper still had half her power, the Charmed Ones would be helpless against the magic of the Dor'chacht. The witches would lose the battle, the last vestiges of their power, and their lives.

And the Dor'chacht would ascend to their rightful place in the universal hierarchy of evil as the feared, omnipotent masters of the mortal world.

Chapter
9

"What day is it?" Paige stumbled into the bathroom, still groggy from sleep.

"Friday." Piper propped her half-awake half sister against the sink counter. Holding Paige steady with one hand, she turned on the water in the tub with the other.

"What time?" Paige swayed on her feet and yawned.

"Time to wake up and help me figure out how to beat the Dor'chacht with almost no powers and two practically useless sisters." Piper didn't try to hide her exasperation.

She had spent the morning helping Phoebe edit pages of scribbled notes into a small memo pad. The process had been complicated by her sister's inability to carry on a meaningful conversation of any duration. The gap in her long-term memory was potentially more dangerous because Phoebe had forgotten the bond of trust they had built with Paige. Piper couldn't even guess how much that, combined with their reduced magic, would affect the Power of Three.

"Useless?" Paige pried one eye open with her thumb and index finger. "It's too early to parry insults."

"I just want to get you motivated." Piper held her hand under the running water to test the temperature. She was tempted to make it ice cold, but decided that she didn't want to deal with a furious witch.

"Okay, I can take a hint." Paige shrugged out from under Piper's hand. "I can also take my own shower."

"Fine." Piper stepped back. "Lunch will be ready when you're done. Then we have to work out a strategy for tonight's magical version of the Hatfields and McCoys."

"Which we don't have much hope of winning." Paige stepped into the tub and pulled the curtain closed.

"Almost none," Piper agreed, choking off a shuddering sob. She had gotten so used to being a whiny woman, the tears had become an irritation she mostly ignored. She couldn't ignore the impending showdown, but it was foolish and dangerous to harbor false hope.

"Not necessarily hopeless, though," Paige said, as though reading Piper's mind. She dropped her robe on the floor and peeked around the curtain.

Piper's glance was unmistakably skeptical. Their chances of winning a battle of dueling spells with weakened powers were poor at best.

"I may only have twenty-five percent of my orbing ability," Paige said, "but considering what it does to coffee cups and candles . . ." An impish grin brightened her face as she left the thought dangling.

An image of the disintegrated objects flashed through Piper's mind. The idea of turning Karen Ashley into pieces and parts was appealing, but not a viable option.

"Except we don't know what powers the evil Ks have locked up in their artifacts along with ours," Piper pointed out.

"We know that Karen's name was Sh'tara and that she was a mind-bender," Paige offered. "And when Leo gets back, we'll probably know exactly what a mind-bender does."

And what powers Kevin and Kate as Tov'reh and Ce'kahn have, Piper thought. *Or will have when they get their powers back.*

"All things considered, it could be worse." Paige flicked the toggle to divert the water pouring from the tap to the showerhead.

Piper didn't want to sabotage Paige's confidence, so she kept silent. Belief in themselves was one of the few positives they had going for them. Unless Leo and the Elders discovered a loophole, chances were better than good that the final round between the Dor'chacht and the Sol'agath would go off as Shen'arch had planned. As Leo had bluntly stated last night, the old Dor'chacht sorcerer had left nothing to chance. He had set up the Sol'agath's ancestors to take a major fall.

Paige stuck her head out from behind the curtain again. "Does our almost complete lack of magic"—she yawned—"make us the innocents in this epic?"

"Beats me." Piper shrugged. As far as she knew, no one else was a player in the family feud. Of course, if the Dor'chacht won, the entire human race would eventually forfeit innocence.

Piper closed the bathroom door and started down the hall feeling as weary as Paige and impossibly more despondent than she had been. She didn't have the strength to deal with her sisters *and* a catastrophe with potential global repercussions. Keeping Paige awake was going to be almost as hard as keeping a coherent dialogue going with Phoebe.

Just as Piper hit the top of the stairs, Paige's high-pitched shriek reverberated through the Manor. Executing an abrupt about-face, Piper dashed back to the bathroom and threw open the door.

"What's the matter?" Piper asked as she burst in, but the answer was immediately obvious.

Paige was at the end of the tub opposite the

tap, wrapped in the shower curtain. Flecks of shampoo lather spattered off her hair as she jiggled up and down, squealing.

Gilbert was at the other end of the tub.

The sight of the grotesque, scaly green beast playing under the spray was so comical, Piper laughed out loud.

"It's not funny!" Clutching the shower curtain, Paige hopped out of the tub. A guttural groan of loathing sounded in her throat.

"Uh . . . yes, it is." Piper laughed again, tears streaming down her face. The frolicking gremlin reminded her of someone who had just discovered the joy of chocolate ice cream. He was deliriously ecstatic.

"*That* is a matter of opinion." Paige shuddered.

Gilbert suddenly realized he was outnumbered two to one and panicked. With a shriek several decibels higher than Paige's, he slithered back into the large faucet. His hefty back legs got stuck for an instant, then vanished into the pipes.

"When did he get so brave?" Piper wiped her eyes, but she continued to chuckle.

"Gosh, I wonder." Paige stuffed the end of a towel into the tap and stepped back into the tub to rinse her hair. "Do you think a sink full of garbage goodies and no apparent intent to capture had anything to do with it?"

"Okay," Piper said, breathing in deeply.

"Guilty as charged, but it's not like Gilbert is the worst thing we have to worry about."

"Easy for you to say." Paige grimaced with disgust. "He didn't plop out of the tap on top of *your* toes."

Piper shrugged, trying not to laugh at the image those words provoked. "Well, he certainly woke you up!"

Paige threw a wet, wadded-up washcloth. It hit the door as Piper jumped back and slammed it closed. Piper didn't regret instigating Paige's angry flare. Even playful flashes of temper would keep her sister's adrenaline going, which might help keep her awake.

Kate stormed into Kevin's apartment. "What's so urgent that it can't wait until we hit the battle-field?"

"What could possibly be more important than attending a strategy session to make sure we win the war?" Karen sat on the sofa with her flute in her lap. She looked back, annoyed.

"House hunting," Kate said. She had been cruising the city trying to decide which mansion she would move into tomorrow. There were so many luxury homes, choosing wasn't easy.

"You can have any building you want," Karen said, "after we defeat the Sol'agath tonight. So let's concentrate on that."

"Sure." As the midnight hour approached,

Kate felt more in touch with her barbaric original self, Ce'kahn, and she was anticipating a rampage of murder and mayhem.

Kate cast a withering glare back at the modern reincarnation of the Dor'chacht warrior, Sh'tara. If Karen did not learn more respect for the empowered keeper of the elements, Ce'kahn would turn the forces of the storm on her after the Charmed Ones were dust.

"Their defeat might be more difficult now, though." Kevin paced the length of the small living room. "Karen wasn't able to touch Piper with the flute last night."

"You failed?" Kate turned accusatory eyes on Karen.

"What was I supposed to do?" Karen sneered. "Reclaim my ability to bend wills just to make sure Piper can't slow us down for a few, inconsequential seconds?"

"And give the Higher Powers the opening they need to send us straight to Hell without a fight?" Kate shook her head. "I don't think so."

"Exactly, Ce'kahn." Karen returned Kate's challenging stare."It's not like they have any chance of winning."

"How can you be so sure?" Kate asked, frowning. She remembered all too well how the Sol'agath's powers and spells had brought them down the last time. Being ripped from her body and cast across time and space had been a terrifying trauma, but the consequences of losing the final round would be far worse.

"Even with their full powers, these witches would be no match for anyone schooled in the customs and magic of the old ways," Karen said. "They are pathetic and puny, the pampered product of a culture that no longer respects the strength and cunning of a warrior."

"I'm certainly glad I've been working out." Since Piper's powers weren't a problem, Kate instantly forgave Karen. She perched on a tall, backless stool by the kitchen counter and pulled a PowerBar out of an opened box.

"It would be a mistake to underestimate them," Kevin said. He faced Karen, his tone sober. "Have you forgotten that we're here *now* because they won then?"

"Really?" Karen walked to the window and looked out.

Kate's gaze focused on the vista of urban canyons visible beyond her sister sorceress. The towering monuments to humanity's technological achievements were vague shadows of significance compared to the ageless buttes, crags, and stone towers of lands long erased from human memory.

Kate was beginning to remember, and her breath caught in her throat as she watched the muscles in the mind-bender's back tense.

Sh'tara had always kept her raw emotions hidden beneath a veil of calm. In this new life, Karen continued to keep contained the seething angers that fueled her power. Soon her ability to command the minds of others would sweep across the world like one of Kate's primal storms, a magical fury that destroyed free will and enslaved everyone she touched.

When Karen slowly turned back around, the detached expression of the cool musician had been replaced by the fierce countenance of a Dor'chacht sorceress. Azure eyes reflected a fire of inner purpose that enflamed the ancient blood in Kate's veins. When they emerged as their true Dor'chacht selves at midnight, all the cultured veneers of modern life would have completely melted away.

Karen's gaze flicked from Kate to Kevin. "If the Sol'agath had *won*, we would not be preparing to meet them in the Valley of Ages to end the conflict now, would we?"

"No, we would not." Kevin met her hard stare with an unwavering control that was not a facade, but the tempered steel of lethal conviction and intent. Shen'arch had put Tov'reh in charge because his sharp mind did not miss the small details and nuances upon which victory so often depended. "But we were not forced to wait three thousand years to avenge our clan because the Sol'agath were weak and powerless. Shen'arch had to use trickery and cunning to arrange this unprecedented chance to undo what has already been decided."

"Nothing was decided!" Karen's temper

erupted. "The instant Shen'arch removed *us* from the field, the outcome was negated."

Kate hadn't thought of it quite that way before, but Karen's words rang true. They did not know with an absolute certainty how the original battle might have ended had they been there with their magic intact.

Closing her eyes, Kate breathed in deeply. The air was alive with the elemental forces she would soon be able to mold into a killing funnel of black wind or a wall of raging water.

"Are you suggesting that Shen'arch acted prematurely," Kevin asked, "before the outcome was sealed?"

"I'm only saying that it's possible," Karen conceded. "We must not doubt ourselves, not for a moment."

"I am Dor'chacht!" Kate slipped off the stool and raised her fist. She could feel the storm she did not yet have the power to call, but the overwhelming connection to it still simmered deep within.

Kevin, too, seemed to sense the magic that was still denied him. He flexed his fingers, anticipating the moment he could turn a log into a dragon or stone into liquid fire.

"All our powers will be restored, while the Sol'agath witches will have almost none," Karen snarled through gritted teeth. "This time, the warriors of darkness will prevail."

• • •

"Guess what?" Piper looked up from *The Book of Shadows*. Her eyes were red with dark circles, but dry.

"What?" Paige stopped pedaling the old exercise bike she had found stashed in a corner of the attic. The activity kept her awake and was infinitely preferable to bathing with Gilbert. Despite the disgusting brush with the gremlin, the gross encounter had produced some unexpected benefits. Now they knew that adrenaline surges countered her fatigue for brief periods, and a good laugh gave Piper momentary relief from her magically induced depression. They were pretty sure that excessive repetition explained why Phoebe could remember her name in spite of having no short-term retention and no memory of ever meeting her.

Phoebe sat in the rocker with the laptop on a small table in front of her. Typing everything into the computer didn't improve her ability to track, but it helped minimize her frustration.

"Did you find something we can use, Piper?" Paige dismounted the stationary bike and stretched.

"Nope. Not a thing." Piper closed *The Book of Shadows* and ran her fingers through her hair. "No charms, spells, or potions. Nothing that will help us defeat the evil blond brigade."

"There must be something we can do!" Phoebe sat back, twirling a strand of hair around her finger. "Wouldn't a Power of Three spell or a potion vanquish"—she leaned forward to read the screen—"the evil Ks?"

"The book says not," Paige said, yawning. She'd have to take a long nap to build up her reserves for the final round, as they were now calling the imminent battle with the Dor'chacht clan. However, all the sleep in the world wouldn't help if they had no means of fighting Kevin, Karen, and Kate's restored magic.

There was no doubt that they'd have a better chance of finding a solution if Phoebe could focus for more than two or three sentences. Phoebe might think of something useful that Paige and Piper had missed.

Phoebe typed something into the laptop, then sat back again, staring at it. "There's no Power of Three spell to vanquish the Dor'chacht."

"Right." Paige exchanged a glance with Piper.

Piper tapped the computer screen. "Just keep reviewing your notes and tell us anything that pops into your head the instant it pops into your head."

"Okay." Frowning, Phoebe turned her attention to the laptop. "We're in big trouble, aren't we?"

"Yep." Piper moved back to the pedestal. She touched *The Book of Shadows*, as though she could conjure an answer to their problems just by wanting it badly enough.

"There's nobody but us standing between this world and one where evil rules," Paige said.

The planet and its human inhabitants weren't

perfect, but most people were mostly good. Only a few, many of whom managed to rise to positions of power, were pure evil. Eventually human good overcame them and the evils they perpetuated, but that was about to change unless they came up with a way to stop it.

"Leo—" Piper started to cry as her White-lighter husband orbed in. "Okay, somebody say something funny before I totally lose it."

One look at Leo's troubled face and Paige's sense of humor took a hike. "Sorry, Piper, but I just can't think funny when my life is on the punch line."

"Me neither," Phoebe said. "I could never remember a punch line when I could remember."

Paige and Phoebe both watched Piper, but their lame attempts to make her laugh fell flat.

"Was there a point to that?" Leo asked.

"Since Piper is still sobbing like it's the end of the world, no." Paige climbed back on the exercise bike and changed the subject. "Judging by the look on your face, Leo, it's a good thing nobody kills the messenger anymore."

"Bad news?" Phoebe nervously chewed her nails.

"It's not good." Leo put his arm around Piper to comfort her, but she just clung to him and cried harder. "Shen'arch made sure that nothing could interfere with the battle tonight, not even the Higher Powers."

"What does that mean exactly?" Paige tightened

her grip on the handlebars to keep from falling off as she fought her own private war with exhaustion. "They can't interfere to stop it? Can't give us a hint how to win? What?"

"They definitely can't interfere," Leo said. "You'll be transported to the Valley of Ages at midnight to finish the feud fight with the Dor'chacht, and nothing on this Earth or in any dimension or plane can stop it."

"Period?" Phoebe asked.

"Exclamation point." Leo pried Piper off his shoulder and eased her down onto one of the large throw pillows on the floor. "I hate to say it, Piper, but maybe it would have been better to let Karen zap you last night."

"How can you say that, Leo?" Piper bawled. She pulled a tissue from the box on the floor, one of several they had placed around the house for her convenience.

"The next emotion might have been anger," Leo explained.

"Which packs a bigger wallop than blubbering," Paige said. "Much handier in a fight, even if we are going in unarmed for all practical purposes."

"At least I've still got half my power." Piper blew her nose and tossed the wadded tissue into a wastebasket. On impulse, she tried to freeze it. As expected, the damp paper stalled in midair for a few seconds, then fluttered to the floor.

On the off chance she had undergone a
miraculous cure in her sleep, Paige tried to orb
the tissue into the basket. She succeeded, but
the paper turned into confetti in the process.

"Where are your powers again?" Phoebe
asked.

"Mine are in Karen's flute," Piper said.

"Kevin's cane." Paige frowned when Phoebe
began to type furiously again. She was curious,
but if she interrupted, Phoebe's thought might
be lost forever. "What about the Ks' powers,
Leo? Any clue there?"

Leo nodded, but his expression was grim.
"As we suspected, Karen can inflict her will on
any being with a mind, Kevin can alter physical
properties of people and things, and Kate con-
trols storm elements."

"We are so doomed." Piper dropped her face
into her hands for a moment and inhaled deeply.
She looked up suddenly. "Aren't we?"

"Doomed?" Leo shook his head. "No. The
battle will take place, but the outcome is not pre-
ordained. That's why Shen'arch arranged the
rematch: to give the Dor'chacht a chance to
change destiny."

"Theirs and ours." Paige pedaled faster, then
slammed on the brakes. "Since when do we go
down without a fight?"

"Since never." Phoebe hit "save."

Piper's misty eyes held an essence of resolve
as she turned to address Paige. "I would love

nothing better than beating the pants off this ancient evil trio, but the odds aren't exactly in our favor."

"Don't underestimate yourselves." Leo twined his fingers with Piper's and squeezed. "You're the Charmed Ones. You can do anything you set your minds to, even if you are the underdog in this fight."

"The underdog *always* wins in the movies." When all eyes turned to stare at her, Phoebe repeated, "Always."

"Yes," Piper said impatiently, "but this is real life, not a—"

"Wait." Paige held up a hand. "She may be onto something. *Why* does the underdog always win in the movies?"

"Because they never give up, not even when the odds are hopelessly stacked against them." Phoebe's enthusiasm was contagious.

"And they make the most of whatever they have," Paige added. "We've been operating on the glass-half-empty principle instead of the other way around."

"Meaning?" Piper frowned.

"I've still *got* twenty-five percent of my orb ability." Paige held up her hand. "It's not as explosive as a blaster, but the results are the same."

Piper nodded as the point struck home. "Half a freeze power is better than no freeze power."

Paige agreed. "Not to mention half a blow-things-up power."

"Especially since Kevin, Karen, and Kate are overconfident," Leo said. "They may actually believe that they're invincible."

"I've got a knack for writing spells, right?" Phoebe's gaze hardened with determination as she pulled her memo pad and pen from her pocket. "And I've got an idea."

Phoebe obviously wanted to contribute, and Paige didn't have the heart to tell her again that no Power of Three spell would vanquish the Dor'chacht's warriors of darkness. However, it couldn't hurt to mention that the movie analogy had changed their perspective for the better. "You probably just gave us a fighting chance we didn't know we had, Phoebe."

"I did?" Phoebe smiled uncertainly. "How?"

"By reminding us that we're the Charmed Ones," Piper said, smiling. "And we always fight back."

Chapter
10

Phoebe grabbed another handful of popcorn from the bowl on the coffee table. A reference on her laptop screen mentioned an automatic transport to a place called the Valley of Ages. Under it she had typed a question: "Similar to Halloween portal to 1670?"

"Are we ready?" Paige asked.

"As ready as we can be, I guess." Piper closed the dusty book Leo had found somewhere in Europe and handed it back to him. She looked at the other tomes scattered around the living room floor and threw up her hands. "This didn't do us a whole lot of good."

"I'll say." Paige sighed. "Apparently, once the evil Ks' essences were whisked into the future by Shen'arch, they were completely off the magical radar. Could there possibly be a reason

we're going into battle without knowing anything except their names and their powers?"

"What we don't know can't hurt us?" Phoebe
suggested.

"I wish." Piper dropped her hands into her
lap. Her lower lip quivered as her gaze swept
over the array of useless research materials. "I
don't know what to look for next."

"I'll have to get these back soon anyway." Leo
glanced at the time. "It's almost dawn in that
part of the world."

Phoebe eyed the stack of ancient scrolls,
books, and manuscripts Leo had "borrowed"
from museums and universities around the
globe. Apparently, as long as he returned them,
his Higher Power bosses didn't consider it
stealing.

"And it's almost midnight here," Paige said.
"I hope Stanley made it back to the shelter."

"Who's Stanley?" Phoebe washed the popcorn down with a swallow of soda and set the
can on the coffee table. She glanced at the short
list displayed on her laptop screen and checked
her pocket for the memo pad. The notes encapsulated everything she needed to know to survive the night.

"A nice old man who is depending on me to
take care of him." Paige smiled sadly. "If I've
done my job right, he'll have a permanent home
at Hawthorne Hill and won't be dependent on
the shelter much longer."

"You haven't heard back on his application yet?" Leo asked.

"No, but it's only been a few days." Paige rolled up a scroll and handed it back to Leo.

"Anything?" In spite of the tears that continuously rolled down her face, Piper cast a hopeful glance at Paige.

"Not much." Paige stifled a yawn. "The only reference I found about disputes between ancient clans mentions 'reversal,' but that's all."

"We already know the Dor'chacht want to reverse how things turned out three thousand years ago." Piper stood up and rubbed her arms. "We just don't know how to stop them from doing it."

Responding to a nagging thought she couldn't grasp, Phoebe took the small spiral pad out of her pocket.

"Then we'd better hope for some instant inspiration, because it's almost time." Paige pointed at the clock.

"Come on, Piper"—Piper gently knocked her fist against her forehead—"think!"

"Hoping to knock some sense into yourself?" Paige asked.

"Maybe," Piper said. "What goes *into* a Dor'chacht artifact must have a way *out* again, right?"

"I've got a spell that reverses a flute." Phoebe held up the memo pad. "Can we use that?"

As Piper started to answer, the living-room walls convulsed and began to fade.

Phoebe stuffed the notebook back into her pocket and jumped up from the sofa. She reached for Piper, but her sister was whisked into a swirling vortex by a powerful, invisible force.

"Leo!" Piper's voice echoed, as though she were falling to the bottom of a deep well.

"Uh-oh." Paige's eyes widened as she was dragged into the maw.

"Paige! Piper!" Phoebe cried out as she was pulled into the swirling cloud of black mist.

Phoebe's stomach heaved with waves of nausea. Hurling through a seemingly endless tunnel of shifting shadows split by tendrils of electric light, she closed her eyes and tried not to panic. An old memory that was still intact surfaced to stabilize her.

She was a Charmed One, one of the three most powerful witches in the world. She had faced worse things than the terrifying forces that held her now.

That thought was swept from her mind as the vortex spit her onto a gray plain dotted with tall, stone buttes and leafless, skeletal trees. Dim light from a full moon cast an eerie, greenish glow on the macabre landscape, and red lightning pierced a bruised, purple sky.

Phoebe scrambled to her feet and brushed off her jeans, wondering if she had just landed in Hell.

• • •

Paige landed on her hands and knees. Sharp stones cut into her palms, and her head swam with waves of dizziness. Disoriented by the turbulent journey, she crawled behind a nearby boulder to compose herself. It took a moment for her eyes to adjust to the twilight that shrouded the bleak terrain.

Twenty feet to Paige's left, Phoebe stood up. Just beyond her, Piper struggled to rise, clutching one arm she must have injured when she was ejected into the Valley of Ages.

The name of this ancient battleground is certainly appropriate, Paige thought with a quick glance around. The desolate terrain looked as though it had been eroded over many millennia. Forbidding and lifeless, the stage mirrored her mood.

In spite of the brave facade she had tried to maintain, Paige felt helpless and vulnerable because her power had been compromised. Considering Shen'arch's ability to mold the elements, time, and space to his magical will, the Dor'chacht warriors of darkness would be formidable opponents even if the Charmed Ones had *all* their abilities.

"Which we don't," Paige muttered. She leaned back against the rough stone and let her eyes droop closed. The exhaustion that had plagued her since Kevin had first touched her with his cane weighed heavier now. Fatigue mingled with utter despair to make surrender seem like the only reasonable course of action.

"If I wasn't a super witch with a family reputation and honor to defend." Paige's eyes snapped open. Willing away the weakness that had seeped into her muscles, she stood up to join her sisters. Together they would face whatever horrors the evil Ks threw at them.

However, Paige thought when the Dor'chacht champions stepped from a portal of churning black ether, *I didn't expect this horror.*

"Who the hell is that?" Piper edged closer to Phoebe.

"The senior citizen or the gruesome three-some?" Phoebe asked.

"Stanley!" Paige groaned, her gaze fastened on the bewildered old man and his Dor'chacht escort.

Stanley was in his stocking feet, with his shirttail flapping over wrinkled trousers. It looked like the warriors of darkness had pulled him from a sound sleep in his cot at the shelter. The old man backed away from his abductors with an expression of undiluted terror.

The only resemblance the three warriors bore to Kevin, Karen, and Kate was the color of their blond hair and blue eyes. During the transition from twenty-first-century San Francisco to the ageless battlefield, they had been cast back into their original forms. Designer jeans, boutique tops, and polished boots had been traded for animal furs, coarse tunics, metal armor, and leather that stank of sweat and blood.

Paige immediately understood the significance of Stanley's presence. "They brought an innocent to distract us, because they know we have to protect him even if it means endangering ourselves."

"Stealing our powers wasn't enough?" Piper asked sarcastically. "That's rather interesting, don't you think?"

Paige definitely thought so. Had the Halliwell ancestors in the Sol'agath clan been so powerful that the Dor'chacht feared them even though they had been stripped of their magic? That question was probably important, but saving Stanley was the priority.

"Kevin knows how much I care about that old man." Paige focused on Stanley and his barbarian captors, trying to quell a surge of guilt. Anything that undermined her confidence and inner strengths was a lethal threat. "I told Kevin all about my interest in Stanley the first night we worked together at the shelter."

"This pathetic excuse for a man is only one of your weaknesses, Paige," Kevin snarled, and shoved Stanley.

The old man stumbled and fell to the ground. He covered his head with his arms, cowering from the monstrous magician Kevin had become.

"Is picking on an old man supposed to impress us?" Phoebe placed her hands on her hips. "Because I've got news: It doesn't."

Considering that Phoebe couldn't remember what was happening or why, Paige was impressed with her feisty attitude.

"You will pay for your insolence, Sol'agath witch." The woman on Kevin's right spoke. Her lip curled to reveal broken, blackened teeth.

Paige recognized Karen by the flute attached to her belt with leather thongs. A tangled mat of hair was held in place by a furred headband adorned with stone and wooden beads. Clusters of beads also hung from thongs that decorated her shield and wrapped around knee-high, furred boots.

"Not if winning smiles count," Piper said.

"How dare you insult me!" Karen lunged.

Kevin's arm whipped out to block her. "Patience, Sh'tara."

"We've been patient long enough!" Kate stood on Kevin's left. Vines and snakeskins were entwined in braided hair that fell past her waist.

Kevin held a sword and a silver-tipped staff, which Paige assumed was the ancient version of his cane. He raised both over his head. "I, Tov'reh, pledge my life, my blood, and my power to vengeance for the Dor'chacht!"

Paige shivered when his cold stare caught her gaze. Although her voice shook when she spoke and her confidence had been rattled, her dedication to duty was steadfast. If she could distract Kevin, maybe she could get Stanley safely out of the line of fire.

"That's a little melodramatic, isn't it, Kevin or Tov'reh or whatever your name is?" Paige cocked her head, deliberately exaggerating the insolence that had infuriated Karen/Sh'tara. Angry people, and hopefully sorcerers, often acted impulsively, which led to miscalculation and mistakes.

"You dare mock me?" Seething with hatred, Kevin drew his sword back.

Paige defiantly stood her ground.

"I am Ce'kahn, and I command the storm!" The impatient and self-centered Kate intruded on Kevin's moment. The bracelet clamped to her forearm gleamed as she thrust her fist at the sky. Her powerful voice rang through the valley as she lowered her arm to place the engraved design against her forehead. "*Guh-sheen toh dak!*"

"Oh, boy," Phoebe murmured.

Piper instinctively raised her hands to prevent Kate from unleashing her powers. The movements of the three Dor'chacht warriors and Stanley were slowed, not frozen.

Kevin's sword slowly descended toward the old man groveling in the dirt before him.

A few seconds was all the time Paige needed. She sprang forward and grabbed Stanley's hand, freeing him from the effects of Piper's slow motion magic. "It's Paige, Mr. Addison. Come with me. Right now."

Stanley's eyes were wide with fear as he peeked from under his arm. His sudden smile was full of relief when he recognized Paige. "Hi, Paige. I'm having a really bad dream."

"Yes, I know." Paige smiled back, tugging the old man to his feet while she watched Kate from the corner of her eye. "Just do what I say, Mr. Addison, and everything will be fine."

"Okay." Stanley clung to Paige's hand and didn't look back as he shuffled after her.

When the slow-mo effect wore off, Kevin shook his sword and roared, railing against the indignity of being thwarted by Piper's partial power. But soon, Paige knew, his anger would be reinforced by his avenging magic. Everyone in and associated with the Sol'agath clan would pay for depriving him of the destiny he believed was his.

Paige glanced over her shoulder as she deposited Stanley behind the same boulder she had used as a shield.

Kate's bracelet glowed crimson and released a red bolt of crackling power, which spread into an enveloping web of pure magical energy. The fiery mesh encased Ce'kahn, flashed, and then dimmed to nothing as the sorceress absorbed her power.

"Stay here until I get back, Mr. Addison," Paige said. "No matter what happens, keep your head down, okay?"

Stanley nodded, then frowned. "What if I wake up?"

"Then you'll be safe and sound." Paige gave him another reassuring smile before she turned away.

Thunder boomed, and Paige's heart pounded heavily against her ribs. The elemental power of the Dor'chacht sorceress, Ce'kahn, was strikingly similar to the power she had possessed in the past as the evil Enchantress. If Leo was right, she would have those abilities again, just not yet.

Which is way too bad, Paige thought. A well-placed earthquake would solve their current problem in a hurry. Instead she'd have to reply on one-quarter orb power and her wits to defeat the enemy.

"*Guh-sheen toh dak!*" Karen repeated the phrase Kate had used to reverse the spell holding the Dor'chacht's powers in their artifacts. She dropped her shield and raised her flute to her mouth, but she did not play. She inhaled the crackling bursts of crimson magic, taking back the power she had relinquished long ago.

Standing on the floor of a bewitched valley with three savage practitioners of the ancient black arts, Paige could no longer think of Kevin, Kate, and Karen by their twenty-first-century names. As each one's power was restored, they became Tov'reh, Ce'kahn, and Sh'tara.

Ce'kahn moved her finger in a zigzag pattern, whipping up a spastic wind to plague the three Charmed witches.

"Now what?" Piper used both hands to keep her windblown hair off her face. A purple bruise blossomed on the arm she had hurt when she had fallen out of the transport tunnel.

Phoebe shrugged. "Darned if I know."

"If we don't do something quick," Piper went on, "it'll be too late to do anything."

"There's something we're missing," Paige shouted back as Tov'reh raised his staff. "It's right on the tip of my mind, but I just can't seem to grasp it."

"Got a hint?" Phoebe pleaded.

"Tell *me*, Paige." Sh'tara's eyes glinted with a wild mania as she glared into Paige's eyes, piercing the barriers into her thoughts.

"Get out! Stop!" Paige screamed, and slapped at her head, frantically trying to dislodge Sh'tara's mental probe. The violation of her mind felt as if her brain were being stabbed with a thousand heated pins. Then it was gone.

"Look at me, Phoebe!" Sh'tara commanded.

Dazed and numb, Paige looked up as Phoebe defiantly met Sh'tara's probing glare.

"What?" Phoebe suddenly clamped her hands to the sides of her face and fell to her knees as the sorceress invaded her thoughts.

Paige realized then that Sh'tara accessed their minds through eye contact. Before she could sound a warning, Piper challenged Sh'tara.

"Leave her alone!" Piper lunged to shove Sh'tara. She reeled backward when the sorceress spun and captured her gaze.

Tov'reh paused to watch Piper writhe under Sh'tara's assault. His hesitation bought a few extra seconds before he, too, reclaimed his old power. It wasn't much time, but Paige used the precious interlude to evaluate the dire situation.

Paige had no doubt that Tov'reh's power to alter the physical state of things would be just as foreboding as Ce'kahn's storm and Sh'tara's ability to force others to her will. She sensed there was a way to beat them, but the elusive solution skittered around her thoughts like a playful puppy that didn't want to be caught just yet.

"They are powerless." Sh'tara's gravelly voice dripped with venomous disdain as she reported her findings to Ce'kahn and Tov'reh. "Except for a warning that helped them identify us, the witches found nothing in their *Book of Shadows* to use against us. There is no spell or charm or potion that can vanquish us."

"Did Shen'arch arrange that, too?" Piper's reddened eyes blazed through a sheen of tears.

If we had *found something useful in* The Book of Shadows, Paige realized, *Sh'tara would now know!*

Something Phoebe had said earlier came rushing back: "What we don't know can't hurt us." Since Sh'tara *couldn't* learn what they *didn't* know, ignorance had protected them from the evil mind-reader.

The deduction was significant, but Paige couldn't consult with Piper without clueing in the Dor'chacht.

"Who are these people?" Phoebe asked, mystified.

"We are your worst nightmare," Ce'kahn said.

"Don't think so," Phoebe quipped. "Although come to think of it, I'm not a big fan of snakes."

"Snakes work for me." Kevin took Phoebe's insult as his cue to act. Dropping his sword, he gripped the staff in two hands and placed the silver end against his forehead.

Paige succumbed to sudden fatigue and closed her eyes, hoping that instant inspiration would strike in the nick of time.

"Guh-sheen toh dak!" The incantation that completed Kevin's conversion into Tov'reh echoed off the cliffs that formed the valley walls.

Paige forced her eyes open as spidery red crackles of magic erupted from the design engraved in the silver end of Tov'reh's staff. Then, suddenly, something Piper said earlier came rushing back: "What goes into a Dor'chacht artifact must have a way out again, right?"

If the Dor'chacht can get their powers back out, Paige thought, *then there must be a way to retrieve ours, too.*

Ce'kahn lifted her arms as though to embrace the sky. "Dark forces of the air and night empowered, this ancient enemy to fell three thousand years agone this hour!"

Thunder rumbled in the distance, and fingers of lightning traced erratic paths across the purplish expanse.

Although inspiration continued to elude her, Paige had another startling insight: She and her sisters *always* seemed to have the tools—potions, spells, charms, whatever—they needed to succeed when they needed them. It didn't make sense that, in this major conflict between magical clans with ultimate good or evil in the mortal world at stake, they would be denied the means to win.

"Your storm confounded and confused the mightiest magics of the old Sol'agath, Ce'kahn, but it's wasted on these feeble modern minds." Sh'tara's pointed gaze turned toward Paige.

Don't look into her eyes! Paige concentrated on a jagged peak on the dark horizon.

"Who are you calling feeble?" Phoebe demanded.

"You will be when I'm through with you," Sh'tara hissed. "Completely and irrevocably mindless."

"That's fine by me," Piper countered. "If we're feebleminded, we won't be terrified. So please, Sh'tara, do us a huge favor and take our free will and our intelligence. Now would be good."

It took a second, but then Paige realized that Piper was gambling on a "briar patch" strategy to trick Sh'tara into leaving their minds alone. In an old folktale, a crafty rabbit had begged a fox *not* to throw him into the briar patch. Unable to resist hurting the rabbit as much as possible, the fox had thrown him into the briar patch, where the rabbit had promptly escaped.

"I don't think so," Sh'tara said, falling for the ploy that matched wit against magic. "I'd rather torment you as long as possible."

"As would I." Tov'reh breathed deeply as the last crimson flickers of magic seeped into his pores. "Beginning with snakes."

"Big, hungry snakes." Ce'kahn pointed at a huge tree. Lightning arrowed downward from a rip in the black clouds that streaked the sky. The bolt hit the base of the tree, felling the timber in a cascade of exploding sparks.

Safe from Sh'tara's mind probes for the moment, Paige desperately tried to piece together the information she was certain she had. As though knowing the immediate danger was passed, her subconscious mind revealed other hints she had said, read, or heard and suppressed.

"The only reference I saw about disputes between ancient clans mentions 'reversal,' but that's all."

Stricken with another surge of intense weariness, Paige swayed. Piper's hand closed on her arm to keep her from keeling over.

"I think we're in trouble," Phoebe said.

"Especially if you have a phobia about snakes," Piper squealed.

". . . the champions of virtue must defend, the light of ages past or be forsaken . . ."

Paige forced her eyes open. Threatened by the storm roiling overhead and Sh'tara's burning brain probes, she had trouble concentrating on the clues she had finally isolated in her mind: ". . . what goes in must come out, reversal, defend the light of ages past . . ." All of it meant something.

"Serpent!" Tov'reh cast the command at the downed tree. The barren branches along the trunk shriveled as the tree morphed into a giant bluish green snake. The reptile slithered directly toward Stanley, who had curled into a fetal ball behind the boulder.

"I think it wants a snack." Ce'kahn waved an arm and a wisp of hurricane-force wind blasted the boulder into a nearby ravine.

The old man curled into a tighter ball, helpless to defend himself.

"Not gonna happen." Paige cast out her hand as the huge reptile opened its fanged mouth to devour Stanley. "Snake!"

"Paige! No!" Piper yelled a warning and shot her hands out to slow the creature.

Paige planted her feet as the serpent's movements slowed. Since her diminished orb took precious seconds to engage, the slow-motion effect of Piper's freeze saved Stanley from a horrendous death. When the massive reptile finally dissolved into millions of orb sparkles, she didn't know if it would disintegrate in transit or materialize to swallow her whole. She just knew she had to protect Stanley.

As the snake's glistening fangs started to reform before her, Paige suddenly realized that the old man was the "light of ages past" the passage in *The Book of Shadows* meant the Charmed Ones to defend.

Stanley Addison's gentle, trusting soul was the light of his past and symbolic of all the innocents the descendants of the Sol'agath clan had protected over the past three thousand years.

Chapter

11

Phoebe watched as Paige turned the snake into a giant sparkler. She loathed reptiles, but this monster was worse than anything she had imagined in childhood dreams. In fact, for a moment she had thought she *was* dreaming!

Piper held her hands out, preparing to freeze the snake when it materialized. "Just *try* to eat my sister, snake!"

"What sister?" Phoebe shuddered and stepped back to pick up a branch that had broken off the tree before it became a voracious viper. She was having a hard time keeping track of the bizarre scenario, but she was certain of one thing: If the fanged monster tried to swallow her, she wasn't going down its throat without a fight.

"*That* sister!" Piper pointed at Paige, then sagged. "Never mind."

Relieved but confused, Phoebe gripped the

branch in the middle like a fighting staff, which felt right. Taking a deep breath, she set her jaw. Paige had deliberately drawn the snake away from an old guy hiding behind a rock. The least she could do was help fight it off.

"You're a fool, witch!" The man called Kevin or Tov'reh, Phoebe wasn't sure which, laughed when the snake began to re-form in front of Paige.

Phoebe held her position when Piper snapped her hands forward to slow the sparkling serpent and the three people dressed like extras in *Conan the Barbarian*.

"*Why* did you do that?" Paige looked annoyed. "The snake will disintegrate before it finishes the orb!"

Before Piper could answer, the barbarians and the snake resumed normal speed.

"You're really making me angry now, Piper!" The savage woman called Sh'tara bared her teeth.

"Like I care?" Piper threw another slow-mo whammy on the three grungy guys and the still sparkling snake.

"I think I know how to get our powers back," Paige said quickly, trying to fit as much discussion as possible into a few seconds. "Just don't look Sh'tara in the eye. That's how she gets into your mind."

"Are you sure?" Piper asked.

"Positive. Each of us locked gazes with her

the last time." Paige cringed when the snake sped up again.

Suddenly the hovering serpent changed from a million particles of light into a million splinters of wood. When it exploded, it had turned back into a tree.

"No!" Tov'reh cried out.

"That works," Piper said, nodding.

"Yeah," Phoebe said, impressed.

"Reverting to type like some people we know." Paige glanced at the furious, fur-clad triplets and smiled with a halfhearted wave at Tov'reh. "Sorry about that."

No, she isn't, Phoebe thought as the tall, muscular man's face furrowed with dark rage.

Tov'reh hefted his staff like a spear, with the ground end aimed at Paige. "You won't be so smug when *all* your power is gone!"

"Piper!" Paige screamed as Tov'reh thrust the staff toward her. It slipped into slow motion mere inches from her throat.

"Okay. Now what?" Piper asked, her hands still extended after throwing the faulty freeze on the staff. "We don't have much time."

"I don't need much." Paige ducked to the side, slid the staff out of Tov'reh's grasp, and reversed it so the ground end was pointing away from her. The sorcerer began to speed up before Paige was back in position, but Piper quickly slowed him and the women again.

"Can I bonk him?" Phoebe was getting tired

of standing on the sidelines doing nothing.

"After I get my powers back." Paige stepped in front of the staff and bent her knees, which lowered her so the engraved silver tip was opposite her forehead. "If this works."

When the Dor'chacht resumed normal movement a second time, the woman called Ce'kahn tilted her head back. "Fire and—"

Phoebe spun abruptly and whacked Ce'kahn in the midriff with the end of the heavy branch, aborting the unfinished command.

"If what works?" Piper slowed the trio a third time so Paige could answer the question.

Ce'kahn slowly doubled over in pain and surprise.

Phoebe grinned. "Not bad."

Paige and Piper were too preoccupied to comment.

"The passage I found about ancient clans and 'reversal' didn't mean reversing how this family feud ended the last time." Paige wrapped her fingers around the engraved silver tip of the staff. "That was just a sneaky way of letting us know we could reverse the power grab, I think."

When Tov'reh came to in the next second, he shrieked with outrage at Piper's audacity, unaware of the changes the witches had imposed.

Paige held on to the silver end of the staff and pressed it against her forehead. "*Guh-sheen toh dak!*"

When Tov'reh realized what was happening,

he tried to yank the staff from Paige's grasp. She didn't let go, but the force of the sorcerer's movement combined with a cosmic imperative that demanded balance in all things jabbed the ground end against his throat. He couldn't break away when small red streaks of magic lightning crackled and sputtered *out* of his pores and back into the staff.

Sparkles of magic flickered off the silver end, too, but they enveloped Paige in a soft blue glow.

"What's happening, Piper?" Phoebe hit Ce'kahn on the head with the branch when she started to straighten. The sorceress staggered backward and bumped into Sh'tara, throwing the mind-reader off balance.

"No time to explain!" Piper looked frantic. "Get Kate's bracelet!"

"Who?" Phoebe couldn't take her eyes off Paige.

Paige's long dark hair billowed around her head as though every strand had been charged with static electricity. Her whole body trembled as blue magic sparkles dissolved into her translucent skin.

"I love fireworks!" The old man sat cross-legged on the ground a short distance away, clapping his hands and laughing.

"Ce'kahn!" Piper waved. "Behind you!"

Phoebe turned just as Ce'kahn caught her around the legs and threw her to the ground. She felt the air rush from her lungs when she hit, and the branch broke into pieces. Dazed and unable to catch her breath, she couldn't roll clear when Ce'kahn straddled her.

"The bracelet!" Piper slowed Ce'kahn and zapped Sh'tara as the mind-reader regained her footing.

Disoriented, Phoebe shook her head to clear a sudden dizziness. She couldn't breathe because a woman moving in slow-mo was sitting astride her, presumably for the purpose of holding her down. From the corner of her eye, she saw Paige jerk a wooden staff away from a blue-eyed, blond guy who was dressed like Attila the Hun.

Piper was running toward her, waving her arms. She started to shout, but another crazed woman decked out in boutique B.C. grabbed her from behind and clamped a hand over her mouth.

An old, shoeless guy with a boyish grin watched the bizarre drama unfold with disturbing calm. He had to be the innocent in whatever supernatural catastrophe the Charmed Ones had fallen into.

Phoebe had no idea why she was lying on her back fighting cave people under a purple sky. Until someone had time to explain, there was only one thing to do: fight.

"Get out of my face, Tov'reh!" With a majestic sweep of her arm, Paige orbed Tov'reh into a thicket of thorny briars and vines. She planted the end of a silver-tipped staff on the ground and hitched her hip to the side, striking a casual pose of triumph. "Who's the fool?"

Phoebe's attention was rudely snapped back to her own predicament when Piper's slow-mo freeze wore off the frenzied woman sitting on top of her.

"*You* will not escape me, Phoebe!" The woman gripped Phoebe's throat in one hand and raised the other. "I am Ce'kahn! Send me fire!"

"The bracelet, Phoebe!" Piper yelled as she broke free of the other woman, but her words were garbled in the gusting wind. "Get her bracelet!"

"Bracelet?" Phoebe asked, and then realized the answer wouldn't matter if she was incinerated by the fireball rocketing toward her from the sky.

Piper knew Phoebe had no idea what was going on or why. However, thanks to Paige's analytical powers, she thought she knew how to get Phoebe's powers and her memory back.

"If she isn't burned to a crisp first," Piper muttered with a glance at Ce'kahn's falling fire-bomb. She snapped her hands toward it, but nothing happened. Apparently, she had used her reduced power so many times in the past several minutes, she didn't have enough magical *oomph* left to slow the flaming missile.

"Fire!" Paige pointed, and orbed the blazing ball toward Sh'tara.

"Rain!" Ce'kahn countered. Instead of being seared, Sh'tara was drenched when a huge globule of water burst.

With her slow-mo freeze on the fritz, Piper had to resort to good old-fashioned nonmagical tactics. Taking heart from Paige's ability to outthink Tov'reh, she ran toward Phoebe. "Grab her arm!"

Phoebe didn't hesitate. Hours of working out with Cole in the Manor basement had left her in peak physical condition, with lightning-fast reflexes. She clamped onto each of Ce'kahn's wrists, wrapped her legs around the woman's middle, and rolled. Holding Ce'kahn's arms in an iron grip, Phoebe planted her knee on the woman's chest.

Piper was amazed at how effective their ordinary human abilities were proving to be against the Dor'chacht's powerful magic. The immobilizing effect of Phoebe's wrestling moves was almost as good as her freeze, when it was functional.

Piper dropped to her knees beside Phoebe and reached for Ce'kahn's bracelet arm. "Can you bend your head down without losing your grip on her?"

"No problem." Phoebe released the bracelet arm and clamped one hand around Ce'kahn's throat while still holding her other wrist.

Just as Piper caught Ce'kahn's free arm in both hands, Sh'tara's sharp fingernails dug into her shoulders. When the mind-reader tried to yank her around, Piper tightened her grip on Ce'kahn and closed her eyes. "Don't look in this one's eyes, Phoebe!"

"Sh'tara!" Paige shouted.

Sh'tara's biting grip dispersed in a shower of orb particles as Paige flung her into a boulder.

"Bend your head, Phoebe." Piper pressed the engraved bracelet design against Phoebe's forehead. Ce'kahn frantically fought to dislodge the opposite side of the metal band, which Piper held against her neck. "Say these words, Phoebe: *Guh-sheen toh dak!*"

"*Guh-sheen toh dak!*" Phoebe inhaled sharply as a cascade of blue sparkles shot from the reddened portion of the design and settled around her like a mist of cool light.

Ce'kahn screamed as red streaks of magic spurted out of her mouth, nose, and eyes into the bracelet.

The power conversion was over in less than a minute. Wind and thunder were silenced, and lightning flashed out, leaving only the moon to light the cloudless gray sky.

Ce'kahn, however, was not quite ready to surrender. When Phoebe stood up, the Dor'chacht sorceress sprang into a crouch. Crazed by hatred and fury, she leaped, her hands held like claws to gouge out Phoebe's eyes. The bracelet slipped off her arm into the dirt as Phoebe levitated out of reach.

Beaten, Ce'kahn collapsed, her power and her spirit spent.

Tov'reh staggered out of the tangle of thorny vines, his face scratched and his eyes dull with defeat.

With Tov'reh and Ce'kahn powerless and Paige and Phoebe's magic restored, Piper was no longer worried about winning the unauthorized rematch with the Dor'chacht. Getting her powers back was *not* a certainty, however.

Piper avoided looking into Sh'tara's eyes as the bedraggled sorceress dragged herself to her feet. She suspected Sh'tara could drive her insane if she had access to her thoughts, but she didn't want to test the theory.

"You may win this war, Sol'agath witch, but the price of victory will be high." Sh'tara's mouth twisted into a cruel smile as she pulled the flute off her belt.

A horrifying thought sent a jolt of nausea rippling through Piper's stomach. Sh'tara's powers had not been neutralized yet. If she had been the last person to touch the flute besides Karen, the instrument's music might still be able to wreck havoc with her emotional equilibrium.

Paige closed ranks with Piper and held out her hand. "Flute!"

"I'm not sure just touching the flute will get

my magic back, Paige," Piper said as the instrument formed in Paige's hand. "Or drain hers."

"Why not?" Paige frowned and absently orbed Sh'tara farther away so the flute couldn't influence Piper and they could talk without being overheard.

The ease with which Paige tossed the sorceress aside enflamed Tov'reh's wounded pride. Although dazed, bruised, and bleeding from his close encounter with the thorny thicket, he barreled toward them with a shriek of maddened fury.

Paige orbed him back into the briar patch. Piper might have found the irony funny if she wasn't so alarmed about her missing powers.

"The three of us can rush Sh'tara and hold her down like you and Phoebe pinned Ce'kahn." Paige grinned. "We just have to be careful not to gaze into her baby blues."

Piper wished it were that simple. She saw Phoebe walking over with her memo pad in hand and decided to wait before she punched holes in Paige's plan.

"And after you've got them," Paige continued, "*you* can blow up the Dor'chacht's powers along with the bracelet, the staff, and the flute. Then that, as they say, will be that."

"And it would probably work," Piper said, "except Karen *played* the flute to drain my powers after I touched it."

"Oh." Paige slumped. "I forgot that she played the flute to commit her magical robbery."

"And we can't force her to play to reverse the process." Piper covered her mouth, but she couldn't stop the sobs. This sadness wasn't a false response to Sh'tara's melancholy music. Her powers were gone, and the pain of loss was unbearable.

On occasion, Piper had cursed the magic and the burdens that came with being a Charmed One, but she would never willingly give it all up, not even if she could have her normal life back. Losing her magic now, after they had thwarted the Dor'chacht's dark vengeance and saved humanity from a darker destiny, just seemed like a cruel, cosmic joke.

"We can't force Sh'tara to play," Phoebe said, "but maybe we can force the flute to play itself."

Piper eyed her younger sister skeptically, hardly daring to hope. "Is your memory back in sync, Phoebe?"

"Regarding the whole family feud in the mystical Valley of Ages program?" Phoebe nodded. "Apparently my updated memory came back with my powers."

"Hey!" Paige blinked. "I'm not tired anymore!"

"Me neither!" Stanley snapped his eyes open. "Am I awake?"

"Oh, no!" Piper gasped. "It's bad enough I'm going to end up being a witch with no magic, but there's no way I can deal with being a weepy wimp the rest of my life."

"I don't think we can deal with that either," Paige quipped.

"We won't have to." Phoebe held up the pad. "Anyone up for a Power of Three spell?"

Paige stole a glance at Piper, as though she was reluctant to crush her hopes. "Sure, but *The Book of Shadows* said there wasn't a spell to vanquish the Dor'chacht."

"Who said anything about vanquishing?" Phoebe grinned. "I don't remember exactly when, but somewhere along the line I had the bright idea to write a spell to make the flute play itself. Apparently I kept one eye on my laptop reminder so I wouldn't completely forget what I was working on."

"Lucky for us!" Paige beamed.

"Lucky for us I *couldn't* remember," Phoebe said, "or Sh'tara would have found out about it with her spooky mind-meld thingie."

"In the attic last night," Piper said, remembering that Phoebe had also mentioned a spell right before they had been witch-napped from the living room, "you said you had an idea, and stupid me didn't bother to follow up."

Paige winced. "I thought she had just forgotten that there wasn't a vanquishing spell, and I didn't want to discourage her from helping."

Sh'tara advanced toward them across the rugged terrain.

"So what's the plan?" Paige asked.

"Tackle, touch, and recite." Piper exhaled. "And since half my power is still in the flute, hope the Power of Two and a Half is enough to get the job done."

"Ready?" Paige gripped the flute tightly.

Phoebe clamped the small memo pad between her teeth.

"Anytime." Piper tensed as Paige held out her free hand and called Sh'tara's name. The startled sorceress suddenly orbed across the remaining distance. The three sisters had her pinned on the ground before she finished re-forming.

"Lean over, Piper!" Paige placed one end of the flute against the struggling Sh'tara's forehead and the mouthpiece against Piper. "Say the words."

"Guh-sheen toh dak!" Piper's voice sounded loud and clear as she spoke the Dor'chacht phrase.

Sh'tara seemed to wither as crackling wisps of red magic spewed from her mouth into the hollow, wooden cylinder.

Holding Sh'tara down with one hand, Phoebe flipped open the memo pad and held it so they could all see. As she began to recite, Paige and Piper joined in.

"Laughing then and crying now, undo this mystic music curse; the Sol'agath command the flute, play Piper's powers in reverse."

As the mellow sound of the flute filled the quiet that had settled over the valley, a blue glow enveloped Piper. The melody had the odd, disjointed cadence of a song being played backward. Piper could feel the sadness lift from her soul and the magic rush back. She laughed once when the backward jig resounded off the cliff walls, and felt an enormous relief when the instrument fell silent again.

"That was a pretty song." Stanley shuffled over.

"Get ready, Piper." Paige hesitated, then tossed the flute into the air. "Testing one, two—"

On three, Piper snapped her hands out.

The wooden flute pulsed with a sudden infusion of molecular velocity. Piper laughed when the cursed instrument disintegrated into sawdust.

"Yes!" Phoebe released Sh'tara and pocketed her pad to high-five the old man.

Thrilled, Piper targeted Tov'reh's staff and Ce'kahn's bracelet. She magically blew them to bits along with the Ks' evil powers.

The ghostly figures of other Dor'chacht fighters and sorcerers suddenly appeared on the ancient battleground. Hundreds of the losing clan were shifted from a long suspension in time through the present on their way to the underworld.

"Do you go to the Fifth Street Shelter, too?" Stanley asked a stately old man with long white hair who had solidified in front of them.

"Shen'arch!" Sh'tara scrambled to her knees

and bowed her head before the ancient master sorcerer. "All is lost."

"*Hoh kan vri-dit?*" Shen'arch's pointed gaze settled on the three witches.

Piper stared back, unwilling to be intimidated by the seething hatred the ancient sorcerer conveyed. Judging by his expression, she guessed that Shen'arch was astounded, appalled, and angered by his dark warriors' failure.

"They were too strong." Sh'tara began to keen in a high-pitched wail.

"And smart," Paige added.

Phoebe nodded. "Resourceful, too."

Piper smiled. Shen'arch's cunning calculations and audacious plan to defeat the Sol'agath had been inspired, but his immense power and manipulations had not been enough. In the end, goodness and the Power of Three had still prevailed.

Shen'arch sagged as the certainty of defeat became apparent to him, too. Tov'reh scrambled back out of the thorny thicket on his hands and knees. Ce'kahn stood up, flapping her arms as though she were trying to chase away a swarm of invisible bees. Then the master sorcerer and his three chosen ones began to change.

Dropping shields and swords, all the Dor'chacht screamed as their magic was removed and released into the void. One by one, their fierce, primitive grandeur was transformed into the grotesque. Long blond and white hair turned to coarse gray tufts of fur, and statuesque bodies shriveled into misshapen, gnomelike forms. Blue eyes became beady black orbs set in wrinkled, brown-spotted faces.

Piper pulled Stanley and her sisters back when a dark maw opened up between them and the diminutive caricatures the Dor'chacht had become.

The black vortex expanded with a deafening roar and scooped the lowercase ks and the rest of their clan into swirling sands. When none but the astonished Charmed Ones and their innocent remained on the valley floor, the violent whirlpool disappeared with a whoosh and a sigh. The moon suddenly vanished below the horizon, and the sun began to rise.

"Is this the ticket home?" Paige asked when a golden light swelled in midair before them. She latched on to Stanley's shirttail as he started to wander away.

"We're about to find out!" Phoebe threw her arms around the group.

"Hang on!" Piper cried when the light irised open and swept them inside.

"Okay," Stanley said.

Chapter

12

Except for the brighter color, the golden light ride home wasn't much of an improvement over the black tornado that had taken them to the Valley of Ages. When she staggered out of the portal back into the living room, Paige's stomach felt like it did on the first dip of a giant roller coaster or when she rode an express elevator down fifty floors: left behind.

"Did everyone make it back okay?" Phoebe asked, counting heads.

Stanley raised his hand. "I'm not sleeping now, am I?"

"No, Mr. Addison, you're awake." Paige let go of his shirttail.

"I need a nap." Without waiting for permission, Stanley flopped onto the sofa. He was snoring before Paige finished covering him with a throw.

Leo and Cole ran in from the kitchen. "You're back!"

"So are you!" Phoebe's smile at seeing Cole lit up the room. "Catch anything?"

"No." Cole embraced her and then gently pushed her back to look into her eyes. "Did you?"

"Just Stanley." Phoebe glanced at the old man. "The Dor'chacht kidnapped him. I guess they thought the distraction of protecting an innocent would give them another advantage over us."

"Apparently it didn't." Leo slipped an arm around Piper's shoulders and squeezed.

"Nope." Piper grinned. "Taking our powers didn't help them either."

"Is Stanley okay?" Leo asked with a worried glance toward the sofa.

"Yeah." Paige gazed down on the old guy for a long moment, then looked up anxiously. "You don't have to worry about him saying anything about what he saw. The magic and everything."

"What did he see?" Leo's worried frown deepened.

"A lot, but he's not exactly . . . coherent," Paige explained. "I mean, if he does say something about whirlpool transports or trees turning into giant snakes, nobody will believe him."

"Trees turning into snakes?" Cole drew Phoebe closer. "That sounds ominous."

"It was," Piper said, "but even though we only had partial powers, we handled it."

"That much is obvious." Leo squeezed Piper again. "You're here, the sun is rising, the Elders didn't sound the emergency alarm, and I'm hungry. Being up all night worrying about you takes a lot out of a guy."

Piper playfully cuffed his arm. "I could use a doughnut."

"I'll buy." Cole held up his car keys.

Phoebe snatched them from his hand. "Wait until I change and I'll go with you. It's been a long five days, and I'm not letting you out of my sight."

"So what finally happened to Kevin, Karen, and Kate?" Leo asked.

"Also known as Tov'reh, Sh'tara, and Ce'kahn." Piper pushed Leo down into a chair and perched on his lap. She lowered her head to his shoulder with a contented sigh.

"Did you vanquish them?" Cole asked.

"Couldn't," Phoebe said. "*The Book of Shadows* was right. There's no vanquishing spell, charm, or potion for the Dor'chacht."

"They didn't get away again, did they?" Cole clarified his interest. "A lot of high-level demons were upset because Shen'arch cheated fate."

"Why would cheating bother demons?" Leo asked.

"In this particular case, it would have set a really bad precedent," Cole said. "Evil thrives on tormenting those who lose in its name. The Dor'chacht haven't suffered for their defeat because they've been suspended in time waiting for this stolen second chance. No one down there wanted them to win."

"They didn't." Paige sprawled in another chair. She diplomatically didn't mention that if Cole hadn't been off fishing, he could have saved them a bunch of time and trouble. Phoebe's ex-demon fiancé was an invaluable source of evil trivia and miscellaneous info.

"The Dor'chacht are finally in the underworld, where they belong." Phoebe grinned.

"So is Gilbert," Leo said.

"We're gremlin free?" Piper sat up. "How'd you manage that, or shouldn't I ask?

Leo's face reddened slightly. "I . . . uh . . . turned off the water to the house for an hour, and he . . . left."

"Just like that?" Paige couldn't believe they had put up with gremlin slime all over the bathroom and gremlin chow in the kitchen sink for days when turning off the water would have solved the problem.

"Just like that," Leo confessed sheepishly.

"How'd you turn off that rusty valve by yourself?" Piper asked.

"I helped." Cole scowled. "After a week in the woods, I was unfit for human company when I got home. I didn't appreciate sharing the shower with our uninvited guest."

"Me neither." Paige cast another annoyed glance at Leo.

Leo countered with more good news. "Mr. Cowan called about fifteen minutes ago, Paige. Doug was worried about Stanley because he didn't show up for lights-out last night."

"I'll call the shelter and let Doug know that everything is fine." Paige sighed, feeling weary in mind and body. The trials of the past several hours added to her job, volunteering at the shelter, being power drained, magically fatigued, and trying to help Stanley had worn her out for real.

"Well, that's not the only reason Mr. Cowan called." Leo smiled. "He wanted you to know right away that Hawthorne Hill Home accepted Stanley. He can move in today."

"Really?" Paige sprang out of her chair and gave Leo a huge hug.

Stanley was probably too exhausted from his adventure to wake up, but Paige knelt by the sofa to tell him the good news anyway. "Guess what, Mr. Addison? You're going to have a new home with a room and your own bed, a shower, and three meals every day."

Stanley rolled over and opened one eye. "Am I dreaming again?"

"No, this is real." Paige's smile faltered when Stanley's placid expression became a disappointed frown. "Is something wrong?"

"No, but—" Stanley sighed. "I want to go

back to that dream so I can see the part where the world eats the ugly little bad people again."

"Yeah, I liked that part too." Paige nodded. Watching the world eat the ugly little bad people was one of the perks of being Charmed.

About the Author

Diana G. Gallagher lives in Florida with her husband, Marty Burke, four dogs, five cats, and a cranky parrot. Before becoming a full-time writer, she made her living in a variety of occupations, including hunter seat equitation instructor, folk musician, and fantasy artist. Best known for her hand-colored prints depicting the doglike activities of *Woof: The House Dragon,* she won a Hugo Award for Best Fan Artist in 1988.

Diana's first science fiction novel, *The Alien Dark,* was published in 1990. Since then, she has written more than forty novels for Simon & Schuster in several series for all age groups, including Star Trek for middle-grade readers, Sabrina the Teenage Witch, Charmed, Buffy the Vampire Slayer, The Secret World of Alex Mack, Are You Afraid of the Dark?, and Salem's Tails. She is currently working on another Charmed novel.